Trevor Holman is English and was born, brought up, and educated in South London, where he worked for many years as a professional musician before moving to Norfolk (which is also in the U.K.). For most of that time, Trevor's career was centered on the music and advertizing industries, while for many years also serving in court as a Magistrate/Justice of the Peace.

In 2003, Trevor and his wife, Frances, moved to the Algarve region of Southern Portugal, where he began a fruitful collaboration with a talented lyricist. Over a six-year period, the two of them wrote in excess of one hundred songs, including four complete stage musicals.

Trevor is now concentrating fulltime on his writing career, and he is currently working on a series of crime novels known collectively as *The Algarve Crime Thrillers*. These novels so far include *The Mijas Murderer*, *The Faro Forger* and *The Salzburg Suicides*, with many more in the series to follow.

The JFK Report however is a one-off "stand-alone" thriller, which takes a behind-the-scenes look at the presidency and the various events leading up to the assassination of John Fitzgerald Kennedy, and the book proposes a new alternative plot as to why it was felt in certain quarters that there was no alternative, and

JFK had to be assassinated. The novel looks at who was really behind it, and who it was that actually carried out the assassination.

Trevor and his wife still live in the Algarve.

This novel is what a lot of people would describe as "faction". A mixture of both fact and fiction, hopefully written in such a way that the reader is not at all sure which is which.

The end result of my efforts is this novel, which is dedicated to all those wonderful people around the world who love a really good conspiracy theory. Enjoy!

Comments made about *The JFK Report* in pre-publication reader reviews

'Trevor Holman has come up with the most preposterous idea yet, and then made it seem entirely feasible.'

'The perfect page turner.'

'The unbelievable – now totally believable.'

'Faction at its best.'

'Frederick Forsyth style narrative, wrapped within Robert Harris style research, and all encompassed in a Dan Brown style plot. Brilliant!'

'Sadly, I really do believe it could have happened – just like this.'

'Wonderful narrative.'

'I could oh so easily believe this!'

'Yet another really great book the Catholic Church will utterly despise, and will no doubt try to get banned.'

'A fantastic idea, fantastically written.'

'This makes far more sense than the Warren Commission's report ever did.'

'It really isn't the Roman Catholic Churches year.'

'I can see the film now, a guaranteed box office hit.'

'This is my kind of book.'

'I don't like it – I love it!'

Trevor Holman

THE JFK REPORT

AUSTIN MACAULEY PUBLISHERS™

LONDON • CAMBRIDGE • NEW YORK • SHARJAH

Ordering Information:
Quantity sales: special discounts are available on quantity purchases by corporations, associations, and others. For details, contact the publisher at the address below.

Publisher's Cataloging-in-Publication data
Holman, Trevor
The JFK Report

ISBN 9781643782126 (Paperback)
ISBN 9781643782133 (Hardback)
ISBN 9781643782140 (Kindle e-book)
ISBN 9781645367352 (ePub e-book)

Library of Congress Control Number: 2019934883

The main category of the book — Fiction / Thrillers / Suspense

www.austinmacauley.com/us

First Published (2019)
Austin Macauley Publishers LLC
40 Wall Street, 28th Floor
New York, NY 10005
USA

mail-usa@austinmacauley.com
+1 (646) 5125767

I would like to thank my wonderful wife, Frances, who never fails to encourage me in all my crazy ideas, including the writing of this particular novel, which I started and completed in just four weeks of non-stop writing during a recent holiday to the States in 2018.

It is my firm belief that I was probably not the best of company during that time, and my apologies go to my long-suffering wife.

Please Note

Many people will tell you that the "Inquisition" is no longer in existence, and that it is just a relic from the Roman Catholic Church's ancient and historic past. This is not true. "Inquisition" still exists to this day; all that has changed is its name.

On the 21st of July, 1542, Pope Paul III proclaimed what is known as the Apostolic Constitution Licet ab initio, establishing a new and powerful organization named the "Supreme Sacred Congregation of the Roman and Universal Inquisition". This new body within the Roman Catholic Church was staffed by cardinals and other officials whose task was defined as being "to maintain and defend the integrity of the faith, and to examine and proscribe errors and false doctrines". The very specific inclusion of the word "proscribe" in this statement by Pope Paul III and the Roman Catholic Church was very deliberate and its meaning was made very clear to every Roman Catholic worldwide. The "Inquisition" had the authority to condemn, denounce, attack and censure. The "Inquisition" was the final court of appeal in all trials of heresy, and the Inquisition's investigations served as an important part of what is known as the Counter-Reformation.

Despite anything you may read or hear, the "Inquisition" has never been abolished by the Vatican, but it certainly disappeared from public view. Because in 1908, after yet another spate of bad "Inquisition" publicity, Pope Pius X decided to rename the "Inquisition" the "Supreme Sacred Congregation of the Holy Office". The Inquisition's name was then changed yet again, for no stated reason, on the 7th of December, 1965. Strangely enough, this occurred very soon after the events described in this book took place. But this time, the change simply removed any reference to the words "Holy Office" and the "Inquisition" was renamed the "Sacred Congregation for the Doctrine of the Faith".

In 1983, everything changed yet again, when the "Code of Canon Law" came into effect. The adjective "sacred" was dropped from the names of all Curial Congregations. And so, what was formally known as the "Inquisition" was yet again renamed, this time to its current name; the very innocent sounding "Congregation for the Doctrine of the Faith".

During the period in which this book is set, the name of the "Inquisition" was still the "Supreme Sacred Congregation of the Holy Office". But in most Catholic countries, this body within a body was at the time simply referred to by everyone as the "Holy Office".

Characters used in the book

John Fitzgerald Kennedy *(JFK)*
President of the United States of America

Jacqueline Kennedy
First Lady of the United States of America and wife of JFK

Robert Kennedy
Younger brother of JFK and US Attorney General

Angelo Giuseppe Roncalli
Pope John XXIII

Giovanni Battista Montini
Pope Paul VI

Cardinal Benedetto Aloisi Masella
Camerlengo to both Popes

Claudio Gabrielli
Head of the Holy Office

Antonio Cavalli
Deputy Head of the Holy Office

Mario Orsini
Gabrielli's senior operative and second in command

Franco Lamberti
Gabrielli's principal gunman

Giuseppe Mancuso
Gabrielli's technical expert

Marco Farina
Gabrielli's lothario

Bernardo Bartelli
Gabrielli's second gunman

Paolo Calico
Gabrielli's third Gunman

Jacques Deangelo
Gabrielli's expert in disguise

Rafael Patressi
Gabrielli's scrounger

Theodore Silvestri
Gabrielli's muscleman

Salvador Mascolla
Gabrielli's muscleman

Nikita Khrushchev
First Secretary of the Communist Party of the Soviet Union.

Patrick Aloysius O'Boyle
Roman Catholic Bishop of Washington

Lee Harvey Oswald
Communist supporter and gunman during the assassination

Jack Ruby
Dallas club owner and killer of Lee Harvey Oswald

Prologue

On November the 22nd, 1963, the 35th President of the United States, John Fitzgerald Kennedy *(more affectionately known to the world as JFK)* was assassinated as he was riding in an open top motorcade along Dealey Plaza in Dallas, Texas. According to the Warren Commission's Report, the 888-page official document presented to Kennedy's successor, President Lyndon B. Johnson, on the 24th of September 1964, President Kennedy had been shot and killed by a lone gunman named Lee Harvey Oswald. According to the report, Oswald was acting completely alone. The self-same Warren Commission Report also concluded that nightclub owner Jack Ruby, who shot and killed Lee Harvey Oswald two days after the accused assassin's arrest, was also apparently acting totally alone.

The majority of people around the world found the final conclusions of the Warren Commission's Report completely incredulous and, quite frankly, totally unbelievable. In fact, the report was soon dubbed "the greatest work of fiction ever published". And so began the hundreds of conspiracy theories that have been discussed, argued about, written about and even turned into films ever since. However, to this day, there has never been a definitive explanation of exactly what happened on Dealey Plaza that has managed to satisfy everyone.

The JFK story started in earnest back in 1960, when the Senator for Massachusetts, John Fitzgerald Kennedy, a young man brought up in an extremely wealthy and privileged Catholic family, decided to run for the office of President of the United States of America. In May of that year, JFK won the Democratic nomination, defeating, in the process, Lyndon

B. Johnson, Senator Hubert Humphrey and Adlai Stevenson. Later that same year, on the 8th of November 1960, John Fitzgerald Kennedy, at the relatively young age of 43, went on to win the White House itself by the narrowest of margins ever. He became the first, last and only Roman Catholic ever to hold the office of President of the United States.

Most people looking on would have thought that having a Roman Catholic President in the White House would have been wonderful news for the Church of Rome. But in the Vatican itself, the current incumbent Pope John XXIII was not at all pleased by the result.

The Pope had already learnt quite a bit about John Fitzgerald Kennedy. He'd made it his business to find out all he could about the Democratic Party's candidate the minute he heard that a Roman Catholic was running for the office of the most powerful man in the world. He commissioned a secret and highly private report into the life, habits and activities of John Fitzgerald Kennedy. Having now read through it several times, he didn't like what was reported back to him one little bit. The problem was simple. John Fitzgerald Kennedy, it appeared, was a totally out of control womanizer. The Pope reasoned that if JFK became the President of the United States, then he would be in the public eye at all times, and Kennedy's extramarital antics and activities would, without any doubt whatsoever, soon become public knowledge. In the Pope's view that, in turn, would undoubtedly bring both disgrace and shame on the Roman Catholic Church.

Pope John's view was very simple; what went on behind closed doors was nobody's business, and the church had always ignored sexual indiscretions of every conceivable type for years. But that was providing they remained totally secret. John Fitzgerald Kennedy, as President of the United States, was about to become the most famous Roman Catholic in the world, apart from the Pope himself, of course. As Pope, he was the undisputed and absolute monarch of the Catholic faith, and the head of the worldwide Roman Catholic Church. His word was law and as he saw it that morning, not only was it his responsibility, it was also, without doubt, his moral duty to protect the good name, teachings, reputation and above all, the moral guidance of the worldwide Roman Catholic Church.

Pope John XXIII made his decision.

Chapter One
November 1960
The Vatican, Rome, Italy

Pope John XXIII, whose birth name was Angelo Giuseppe Roncalli, arrived in this world on the 25th of November, 1881. Now, as Pope, he had become the head of the Catholic Church and ruler of the Vatican City State from the 28th of October 1958 onwards. Angelo Giuseppe Roncalli was born the fourth of fourteen children. He arrived into a fairly poor family of sharecroppers who lived in a village in Lombardy. He was ordained as a priest in August 1904, and held several posts, including that of nuncio in France, and then becoming a delegate to Bulgaria, Greece, and Turkey. In a consistory, which in the Catholic church is the official title of the council of cardinals, meeting on the 12th of January 1953, the then Pope Pius XII made Roncalli a Cardinal and named him as the Patriarch of Venice.

The election of a new Pope occurs soon after the current occupant of the post has died, at a special meeting to which the 'College of Cardinals' *(i.e. all the world's Roman Catholic Cardinals)* are required to attend. This meeting is known as "Conclave" and it begins when all the Cardinals are locked inside the Sistine Chapel where they cannot be disturbed or influenced by outside pressures until a new Pope has been elected. The outside world is kept informed of what is going on inside Conclave by the sending up of either black smoke *(to indicate a failed ballot with no new Pope being elected)* or white smoke which tells the world that a new Pope has successfully been chosen. The sending up of both the black and the white smoke is done through a special chimney, the base of which is located inside the Sistine Chapel. The new Pope is then declared by the Catholic Church to be God's own choice, and his election is therefore deemed to be God's will. The Cardinals do their bit in this procedure by discussing the merits of those Cardinals up for election, and then casting ballots until a winner is finally declared. If they fail to reach agreement, black smoke is sent up the chimney, and the discussions start again. In Cardinal Roncalli's case, it seemed they were either not aware of God's will or sadly, it had not been made very clear to all the Cardinals to say the least, as it took them eleven different ballots before he was finally elected Pope on the 28th of October 1958 at the age of 76. His selection was to say the least, most unexpected, especially to Cardinal Roncalli himself, who had come to Rome for Conclave with a return train ticket to Venice in his pocket.

According to Roman Catholic teaching, and this is only true of Roman Catholic teaching, the history of the Catholic Church begins with Jesus Christ himself and his teachings. Jesus lived in the Roman province of Judea and he was born in Bethlehem in approximately 4BC. His family fled to Egypt and they subsequently returned to Nazareth in Galilee approximately a year later. Galilee and the surrounding area were conquered by the Roman Empire in 6AD, becoming part of the province of Judea. According to Roman Catholic teaching, the Roman Catholic Church is the continuation of the early Christian community established by Jesus Christ himself. And as the Catholic Church teaches, its bishops are the successors to Jesus's apostles and the Bishop of Rome, known to most people as the Pope, and he is the sole successor to Saint Peter who was appointed by Jesus as head of the church in the New Testament, and is ministered in Rome. By the end of the second century, bishops began congregating in various regional synods to resolve doctrinal and policy issues. By the third century, the Pope began to act as a court of appeals for problems that other bishops could not resolve themselves.

Christianity spread throughout the early Roman Empire, despite persecutions due to conflicts with the pagan state religion. Then, in 313AD, the struggles of the early Church were lessened by the legalization of Christianity by the Emperor Constantine I. In 380AD, under the Emperor Theodosius I, Catholicism became the state religion of the Roman Empire by the decree of the Emperor himself, which would persist until the fall of the Western Empire and later, with the Eastern Roman Empire until the Fall of Constantinople. During this time, the period of the Seven Ecumenical Councils, there were considered five primary sees, or if you prefer, five main jurisdictions within the Catholic Church. These five, known as the Pentarchy were Rome, Antioch, Constantinople, Alexandria and Jerusalem.

The battles of Toulouse preserved the Catholic west, even though Rome itself was ravaged in AD850 and Constantinople was besieged. Then in the eleventh century, the already-strained relations between the primarily Greek church in the East, and the Latin church in the West developed into the East-West Schism, partially due to conflicts over Papal Authority. The fourth crusade, and the sacking of Constantinople by renegade crusaders, proved the final breach. Prior to and during the sixteenth century, the Church engaged in a process of reform and renewal. Reform during the sixteenth century is now known as the Counter-Reformation. In subsequent centuries, Catholicism spread widely across the world despite experiencing a reduction in its hold on European populations due to the growth of Protestantism, and also because of massive religious skepticism both during and after what is known as the Enlightenment. The Second Vatican Council, in the 1960s, introduced the most significant changes to Catholic practices since the Council of Trent, four centuries before.

To put it simply, and again, to emphasize only according to Roman Catholic teaching, the Roman Catholic Church was founded by Jesus Christ. The New Testament records that Jesus appointed twelve Apostles and his instructions to them were to continue his work. The Catholic Church teaches that the coming of the Holy Spirit upon the apostles, in an event known as Pentecost, signaled the beginning of the public ministry of the Church. Roman Catholics hold that Saint Peter was Rome's first bishop, or Pope, and he was the consecrator of Linus as its next bishop, thus starting the unbroken line which includes the current pontiff or pope. That is, the Roman Catholic Church maintains the apostolic succession of the Pope as the successor to Saint Peter. Pope John XXIII, who was reportedly described by several Cardinals during Conclave as being "a bit too rotund" had been Pope for just over two years. He was now extremely comfortable and settled in the role he had taken on. He sat in his private office, leaned back in his chair and switched off his TV set. He had been watching the news and had just heard that the United States of America had elected its first Roman Catholic President, a young 43-year-old man named John Fitzgerald Kennedy. He let out a huge sigh, picked up the telephone on his desk and spoke to the operator.

'Can you find Camerlengo Masella for me please, and have him come to my office straight away. Thank you.' Pope John XXIII was always polite on the telephone.

'Of course, Holy Father,' the operator replied. The Pope replaced the telephone on its cradle and sat staring at the blank TV screen, deep in thought. He'd hoped this problem would not have arisen and if Richard Nixon had only beaten Kennedy then he would not be facing the problem he was dreading having to deal with. But deal with it he must. There was a gentle knock on the door and his old friend of many years and his trusted "Camerlengo" Cardinal Benedetto Aloisi Masella entered his office.

In the Vatican, the position of Camerlengo is more or less what the outside world would call the Pope's PA, and quite often, he is also his closest confidante. The role, or office of Camerlengo is without doubt one of the most important and influential in the Catholic Church as the Camerlengo is one of the very few people who have direct access to the Pope. Cardinal Masella was chosen for this very important role on the 9th of October 1958 by the "Curial Cardinals" (the previous Camerlengo having resigned). The post had been empty during the reign of Pope Pius XII, who had been Pope for the previous 20 years. For his own unknown reasons, he had failed to appoint a new Camerlengo before his death, but the rules stated that a Camerlengo was needed to arrange and supervise Conclave. Cardinal Benedetto Aloisi Masella was given the job. Pope John looked up, smiled at his good friend of many years and indicated with his arm that the door should be closed.

'Have you seen the news this morning, Benedetto?' he asked.

'You mean about Kennedy?' the Camerlengo replied. 'Yes indeed, what wonderful news. At last, a Roman Catholic President in America.'

'No, my friend, I'm afraid it's not so wonderful,' said the Pope. Cardinal Masella sat down in the chair in front of the Pope's desk with a curious look on his face, now wondering about the strange comment the Pope, and his good friend, had just made. Pope John reached down and slid open the top right-hand drawer of his massive mahogany desk and pulled out an A4 size beige-colored folder. He held it out for the Cardinal to take.

'Please, Benedetto, read the contents of this file thoroughly, and then tell me it is wonderful news.'

The Camerlengo reached out, took the file, opened it and started to read. Every now and again, Cardinal Masella looked up from the report and was about to make a comment, but Pope John waved his hand to indicate he should keep reading and say nothing until he'd finished. He bent his head of white hair forward and went back to reading the report. When he'd eventually finished, he looked up and asked,

'If you don't mind me asking, Holy Father, who wrote this report, should we believe everything it says, and most importantly, do you believe the conclusion drawn at the end?'

'Two things, Benedetto. Firstly, when we are in this office and the door is closed, I am your friend of many years, and please call me by the name you used all that time, Angelo.

Secondly, yes, unfortunately, I believe every word of the report. I personally commissioned the investigation when Kennedy won the Democratic nomination. Since then, I have been receiving regular updates from reliable sources in America, and sadly, I have to agree with the report's dire conclusions.'

'But if what the report concludes is the case,' said Cardinal Masella, 'the Catholic Church is potentially facing the biggest crisis in its history.'

Chapter Two
January 1961
The White House, Washington D.C.

Newly elected President John F. Kennedy sat in the big swivel chair behind the large desk in the Oval Office, and spun around in it like a child playing on a roundabout. The only other person in the room with him was his younger brother, Bobby.

'For God's sake, Jack, don't break the damn chair on your first day.'

Although his first name was John, the man that became known to the world as JFK had always been called Jack by his family and friends.

'We damn well did it, Bobby,' the new President giggled. 'I just can't believe that we won the damned election, even though we only won 22 states and that wretched man Richard bloody Nixon won 26.'

'Yes,' replied Bobby. 'That's true, but it really doesn't matter, Jack; it is history now. The most important thing is that you won the popular vote, and that's what counts, even if it was by a margin of only 0.1%.'

'Oh, forget all that,' replied Jack. 'As you say, it's over and done with. The most important thing is we're here, in the White House, and from now on, we make all the decisions. At long last, we can turn the USA into a force for good.'

'You mean you can, Jack,' corrected Bobby.

'No, Bobby, I mean us,' said Jack. 'It's going to be the same as it's always been, you and me together. I am announcing today that you have been appointed the 64th United States Attorney General with immediate effect.'

'Are you sure about that, Jack?' questioned Bobby. 'Obviously I'd love to do it, but everyone will say it is pure and simple nepotism.'

'Who cares? As far as I'm concerned, you are exactly the right man for the job. You bravely served your country in the U.S. Naval Reserve during the Second World War, you later graduated from Harvard, receiving your law degree from the University of Virginia before being admitted to the bar. You were the assistant counsel to the Senate Committee chaired by Senator Joe McCarthy, plus you took on Jimmy Hoffa and the Teamsters Union. None of that has anything to do with nepotism; that's just a list of facts that nobody can dispute, and anyway, screw them all, Bobby. If they don't like it, they can damn well lump it. As of now, you are the new U.S. Attorney General. End of story.'

The two of them laughed, just as there was a quiet knock on the door, which neither of the brothers heard due to their laughter. This was quickly followed by a louder knock which they did hear, and Jack called for whoever it was to come in. The person that entered was Evelyn Maurine Norton Lincoln. She was a 51-year-old, happily married woman who had faithfully served as Jack's personal secretary since his election to the United States Senate, way back in 1953.

'I have a Cardinal Masella on the telephone for you, Mr. President,' she said. 'The Cardinal said he is calling from the Vatican.'

'Probably wants to congratulate you, Jack,' said Bobby.

'Put him through, will you please, Evelyn,' said Jack as he sat forward. He took the telephone receiver off its cradle, and held it to his left ear.

'Good morning, Mr. President,' he began. 'I am Cardinal Masella, the Holy Father's Camerlengo, and both he and I wish to congratulate you on achieving such high office, and at so young an age as well.'

'Well, thank you,' replied Jack. 'And please thank the Holy Father for me, for both his and your own kind wishes.'

'I will, of course. The Holy Father also has a small request, Mr. President. He would be most grateful if you would graciously accept a short visit from Bishop O'Boyle at your earliest convenience?'

'I'm sure that can be arranged with my personal secretary, your eminence,' replied Jack. 'But can you give me some indication of the reason for the Bishop's visit?'

'The Bishop will explain when he sees you, Mr. President, and can I thank you for your kindness in agreeing to see Bishop O'Boyle? I will disturb you no longer, and I will also make all the necessary arrangements straight away with Mrs. Lincoln. Once again, many congratulations on your excellent election victory.'

With that, the phone went dead.

'Well, that was really strange,' said Bobby. 'I wonder what this Bishop O'Boyle character wants. Do you know him?'

'I haven't a clue who he is,' said Jack. 'Or what he could want, but no doubt we'll find out in due course. Look into him for me, Bobby, will you? I like to know who I'm talking to.' With that, Jack started laughing as he began spinning round in the chair again.

Chapter Three
January 1961
The Vatican, Rome, Italy

'Did you manage to clearly explain the situation to Bishop O'Boyle?' asked Pope John. 'And are you one hundred percent sure he totally understood what is being asked of him, and just how important this is?'

'Oh he fully understands, all right,' replied the Camerlengo. 'I spent nearly an hour on the telephone with him, including reading most of your report to him. He is, I promise you, as equally worried about the possible consequences for the church as we are, and he has assured me he will make sure President Kennedy fully understands what must be done.'

'He must understand, Benedetto,' said the Pope. 'This is not a matter for debate. Kennedy must accept our position and obey the instructions of his Pope. He is a full member of the Roman Catholic Church and I will not, under any circumstances, tolerate any unwillingness on his part to cooperate with my wishes.'

'I agree with you wholeheartedly, Angelo, but what do we do if he decides to ignore your wishes? He is no longer just an ordinary Catholic; he is now the President of the United States and he may feel he is above your wishes. What do we do then?'

'I fear we will be left with no choice, Benedetto. We will have to call in the Supreme Sacred Congregation of the Holy Office, and they can deal with him,' replied Pope John.

'Isn't that a bit extreme, Angelo? I know the name changed back in 1908, but in reality, they are still the same. Are you really saying you will call in the Inquisition?

'What do you suggest I do? Let this man run wild like a loose cannon, and let him bring down the largest church in the world? Our church? No. It is not his choice, and he must, at all costs, be stopped. Bishop O'Boyle must make it very clear to America's new president that as a Roman Catholic, he cannot just do what he wants in life.'

'Do you want to speak to the Bishop before he meets with President Kennedy?' asked the Camerlengo.

'No,' replied the Pope. 'He knows exactly what I want. Let us just pray that President Kennedy will understand the church's position and see sense.'

Chapter Four

January 1961
The White House, Washington D.C.

The Kennedy family originated from the Ó Cinnéide Fionn, one of the three Irish Gaelic Ó Cinnéide clans who ruled the kingdom of Ormond. Their progenitor, Diarmaid Ó Cinnéide Fionn, held Knight Castle close to what is today Puckane, County Tipperary, in 1546. From there, having lost out to the New English order in the Kingdom of Ireland, they ended up in Dunganstown, New Ross, County Wexford by 1740, and it is here that Patrick Kennedy was born in 1823.

The first Kennedys to reside in the United States were Patrick Kennedy and Bridget Murphy, who sailed from Ireland to East Boston in 1849. Patrick worked in East Boston as a barrel maker, or cooper, and he and Bridget had five children. Their youngest, Patrick Joseph, or "PJ Kennedy", went into business and served in the state legislature.

PJ and Mary Augusta Hickey were the parents of four children. Their oldest was Joseph Patrick 'Joe' Kennedy Senior, who amassed a fortune in banking and securities trading, which he further expanded by investing in other growing industries. Joseph Senior was appointed by President Franklin D. Roosevelt as the first chairman of the Securities and Exchange Commission, chairman of the Maritime Commission, and he was the U.S. Ambassador to the United Kingdom in the lead up to World War Two. He served on the Commission on Organization of the Executive Branch of the Government from 1947 to 1949, which was appointed by President Truman to recommend administrative changes in the federal government.

Joseph Senior and Rose Elizabeth Fitzgerald were, in total, the parents of nine children. Joseph Jr., John, Rosemary, Kathleen, Eunice, Patricia, Robert, Jean and Edward, who was known to most people as "Ted". Joseph Sr. had expected his eldest son, Joseph Jr., to go into politics and ultimately be elected President. But after Joseph Jr. was killed during World War Two, Joseph Senior's expectations transferred to his second son, John, who was now known to everybody as Jack.

Jack and Bobby were seated opposite each other on a couple of sofas in the Oval Office, waiting for the imminent arrival of Bishop O'Boyle.

'So, fill me in, Bobby. What do we know about this Bishop?' asked Jack.

'His full name,' answered Bobby, 'is Patrick Aloysius O'Boyle, and he was born on July 18, 1896, in the town of Scranton, in Pennsylvania. His parents are Michael and Mary O'Boyle, a couple of Irish immigrants. His father was originally from County Donegal, and he came to the United States in 1889, where he settled in New York. Bishop O'Boyle's mother moved to New York from County Mayo in 1879, and later married his father in December 1893. Shortly afterwards, they moved to Scranton, where the father became a steelworker. They also had a daughter, but she died during infancy in 1895. O'Boyle began his studies for the priesthood at St. Joseph's Seminary in New York, and was ordained a priest by Archbishop Patrick Joseph Hayes on the 21st of May, 1921. Patrick Aloysius O'Boyle was appointed a Bishop, taking office in 1948 and, according to my sources, he is likely to be elevated to Archbishop fairly soon, and then the Cardinalate in the not too distant future.'

'The what?' asked Jack.

'Cardinalate,' replied Bobby. 'Basically, they're quite likely to promote him to Archbishop of Washington, and then make him a full Cardinal fairly soon after that, unless, of course, he screws up somehow.'

There was a loud knock on the door and without waiting for a response, Evelyn opened the door and showed Bishop O'Boyle into the Oval Office. Jack and Bobby both stood, and walked forward to greet him, holding out their right hands. 'Good morning, Your Excellency,' said Jack. 'This is my brother, Bobby, who also happens to be the United States Attorney General.'

'Good morning, gentlemen, and thank you for seeing me.' Bishop O'Boyle shook both of their hands and then sat in the armchair Jack indicated to him that was positioned between the two sofas. Jack and Bobby sat back opposite each other on the two sofas so that the three men now formed three sides of a square.

'What can we do for you, Bishop?' asked Jack, getting straight to the point.

'This is a little delicate, I'm afraid, Mr. President, but may I start by assuring you that my words come directly from the Holy Father, and they are not my own. Indeed, my mission in seeing you today is that of the utmost importance to the Holy Father, and it is he that has asked me to broach this somewhat delicate matter with you.'

'I see,' said Jack warily. 'I think. And what, may I ask, exactly is this somewhat delicate matter you are referring to, Bishop?'

The Bishop held back for a moment or two as he assembled the words in his brain before speaking. When he did speak, it was in a quiet, but authoritative, tone. 'It has come to the Holy Father's attention, Mr. President, that despite your being a married man with children, you have certain tendencies relating to members of the opposite sex which are not appropriate for a married man, but even more so, not in the least bit appropriate for a Roman Catholic with a high public profile, which you most certainly now have.'

'My God, Jack,' laughed Bobby. 'You're getting chastised by the Pope for your dalliances with young ladies other than Jackie.'

'I see you find this most amusing, Mr. Attorney General, but I'm afraid the Holy Father does not, and he has instructed

29

me to make sure the President understands just how seriously Pope John views this matter. He feels that a Catholic President has a responsibility to act in a suitable manner that would not bring shame on his church. The Holy Father feels he has no choice but to insist that as a prominent member of the Roman Catholic Church, your sexual activities can do nothing other than bring shame, disgrace and dishonor to the good name of the church, and as such, the Holy Father has instructed that all such behavior by you must cease with immediate effect, and you must from now on and at all times conduct yourself in a respectful manner according to the laws and morals of the church.'

'Let me get this straight, Bishop,' said Jack. 'Are you sitting here in the Oval Office of the White House, telling the President of the United States what he can and can't do in his own personal and private life?'

'No, Mr. President, I am not telling you that. The Holy Father as Pope and Head of the worldwide Roman Catholic Church to which you belong is telling you that.'

Jack stood up indicating that as far as he was concerned, the meeting was over. 'Please understand me, and understand me well, Bishop,' said Jack. 'When I stood for election as the Democratic Party's candidate, I stated very clearly at the convention on September the 12th, back in 1960, 'I am not the Catholic candidate for president. I am the Democratic Party candidate for president who also happens to be a Catholic. I do not speak for my Church on public matters, and the Church does not speak for me.' I repeat that to you now, Bishop. 'The Church does not speak for me.' Please inform the Holy Father,' continued Jack, 'that I have most certainly heard his words, but the President of the United States is not a pawn of the Pope, and he will not kowtow to him and meekly do his bidding. I will live my life in the way I see fit. For both yours and his information, I love my wife and both of my children, and I will not have someone who has never met me, or for that matter, someone who has never even spoken to me, no matter what his position, tell me what I can and can't do in my own private life. Do you think you can remember all that, Bishop?'

'Oh, I can remember every word, Mr. President,' replied Bishop O'Boyle. 'I just pray that you will not live to regret them.'

Chapter Five

January 1961
The Vatican, Rome, Italy

After Bishop O'Boyle had left the White House, he went straight back to his home in Washington D.C., packed a suitcase and headed to the airport where he caught the next available flight to Rome. The following day, he was admitted into the Pope's private office in the Vatican by Camerlengo Cardinal Masella, and the three men then sat down around the Pope's desk.

'I gather, from what the Camerlengo has already told me,' began Pope John 'that President Kennedy was not at all receptive to my message?'

'You could say that, Holy Father,' replied the Bishop. 'I made it very clear to him that as a prominent Roman Catholic, it was his responsibility to act in a suitable manner that would not bring shame on the church. His response was totally negative and, if I'm honest, somewhat aggressive. In reality, he basically threw me out.' Bishop O'Boyle then went on to reiterate every word that had been spoken in the Oval Office including President Kennedy's comments at the end.

'I see,' said Pope John, frowning.

'You think there is no reasoning with him?' asked the Camerlengo.

'No,' replied Bishop O'Boyle. 'I believe both President Kennedy and his younger brother, who he has now made the U.S. Attorney General, have already let their newfound power go to their heads. I honestly think they both believe they can do and say whatever they want, and there will be no consequences.'

'Oh, there will be consequences,' muttered the Pope to himself.

Bishop O'Boyle left the Pope's private office half an hour later, the three men having discussed various possible ways in which they might get through to the President, and make him see that his behavior would reflect badly on the church. But sadly, they could see no light at the end of the tunnel. Once the Bishop had left, the Pope picked up his telephone.

'Please get me Signor Claudio Gabrielli at the Supreme Sacred Congregation of the Holy Office.' The Pope continued to hold the phone while he waited to be connected. 'Please understand me, Benedetto, I would prefer not to go down this route, but I am afraid President Kennedy has left me with no choice. Signor Gabrielli is a good man, and I'm sure he will understand the situation and know how to deal with it.'

At that moment, Claudio Gabrielli came to the phone. 'Holy Father, what an honor. How can I be of service to you?'

'Signor Gabrielli, I have a small problem I think you can help me with. Could you please come to my office in my private quarters straight away, and I will explain what is needed of you?'

'Of course, Holy Father,' replied a thrilled Gabrielli. 'I am on my way.'

Formerly known as the "Supreme Sacred Congregation of the Roman and Universal Inquisition", the "Supreme Sacred Congregation of the Holy Office" is now informally known in most Catholic countries simply as the "Holy Office". But to most people who knew about this organization within an organization, it may have changed its name, but it was still the "Inquisition". Founded by Pope Paul III in 1542, the Holy Office or Inquisition's principle aim, and its official objective is to "spread sound Catholic doctrine and defend those points of Christian tradition which seem in danger because of new and unacceptable doctrines". This had always been the case throughout the history of the Roman Catholic Church's Inquisition, irrespective of what name it went by.

The Catholic Church has been criticized over the years for several of its edicts, many of its rules and practices, but most often for not practicing the Christian love it preaches.

Beginning in the 19th century for example, historians have gradually compiled statistics drawn from the surviving court records. Study of the records of the Spanish Inquisition alone lists 44,674 trials of which 826 resulted in executions of the person, and in 778 cases in effigy, in which a straw dummy was burned in place of the person as an example to the crowds. Historians have also estimated that there were over 1,000 executions between 1530 and 1630 and a further 250 between 1630 and 1730. Studies of the records of Toledo's tribunal alone, for example, show over 12,000 people were put on trial. For the period prior to 1530, it is estimated there were over 2,000 executions in Spain's tribunals. All of these things were done by the inquisition in the name of the "not so loving" Roman Catholic Church.

Then there was the practice of "Indulgences". In the teachings of the Roman Catholic Church, an indulgence was a way to reduce the amount of punishment someone has to undergo for their sins. It may reduce the temporal punishment for sin after death for example, as opposed to the harsh eternal punishment merited by committing a mortal sin, in the state or process of purification called Purgatory. The Catechism of the Catholic Church describes an indulgence as "a remission before God of the temporal punishment due to sins whose guilt has already been forgiven, which the faithful Christian who is duly disposed gains under certain prescribed conditions through the action of the Church which, as the minister of redemption, dispenses and applies with authority the treasury of the satisfactions of Christ and the saints". The recipient of an indulgence must perform an action to receive it. These days, this is most often the saying (*either once, or many times*) of a specified prayer, but it may also include the visiting of a particular place, or the performance of specific good works.

Indulgences were originally introduced by the Catholic Church for two reasons. Firstly, for the remission of the severe level of penances dished out by the early Church, which were often granted to Christians awaiting martyrdom or at least imprisonment for the faith. Secondly, however, by the late Middle Ages, indulgences and the granting of them was mostly in exchange for monetary payment as such indulgences had become a massive source of income for the Catholic Church and its priests. This clerical abuse of indulgences, mainly through commercialization, had become a serious problem which the Church recognized but try though it might, was unable to restrain. Its priests were effectively running wild and happily lining their own pockets in the process. Indulgences were, from the beginning of the new Protestant Reformation, a target of attacks by Martin Luther and all the other Protestant theologians of the time. Eventually, the Roman Catholic Counter-Reformation curbed the excesses, but indulgences still continue to play a role in modern Catholic religious life. Reforms in the 20th century largely abolished the financial aspects of indulgences, and the quantification of indulgences, which had previously been expressed in terms of days or years. These days or years were meant to represent the equivalent of time spent in penance, although it was widely taken by those buying indulgences to mean time spent in Purgatory.

Another criticism of the Catholic Church is the horrendous historical killings carried out in the church's name in South America during the conquistador period. These are a fact of history, and the Roman Catholic Church can do nothing to change history, as much as it may wish it could. But for most people, the biggest criticism of the modern Catholic Church is the firm belief that it is rich beyond compare, with a massive quantity of incredibly valuable treasures safely stored away, plus mountains of both cash and gold sitting in the Vatican's vaults, while millions of the churches members around the world are suffering poverty and starvation.

These various criticisms had and have been going on for centuries, and the organization within an organization frequently charged with dealing with the public perception of the church was the "Holy Office", and that was currently headed up by the man now heading to see the Pope; Signor Claudio Gabrielli.

The home and headquarters of the 'Holy Office' are in the "Palace of the Holy Office", which is located just outside Vatican City; a building in Rome which is an extraterritorial property of Vatican City. The palace is situated south of St. Peter's Basilica near the Petriano Entrance to Vatican City. The building lies outside the confines of Vatican City at the south-eastern corner of the city-state. It is one of the properties of the Holy See in Italy, regulated by the 1929 Lateran Treaty signed with the Kingdom of Italy. As such, it has extraterritorial status.

The palace was first built after 1514 for Cardinal Lorenzo Pucci, and it was called Palazzo Pucci. Its façade was rebuilt in 1524 by the architects Giuliano Leni, Pietro Roselli and the great Michelangelo. When Pucci died in 1531, the building was still not fully completed. In 1566, the palace was purchased by Pope Pius V for 9,000 scudi, and it was converted into the seat of the Holy Office. Vast renovation works were undertaken by Pirro Ligorio and Giovanni Sallustio Peruzzi and then, between 1921 and 1925, a complete renovation of the building was made by Pietro Guidi.

The role of the 'Supreme Sacred Congregation of the Holy Office' as defined by the Pope is to "promote and safeguard the doctrine on faith and morals in the whole Catholic world", and as such it has the right to involve itself in any and all things that touch this matter in any way. That's a pretty vague description, which basically means they have the right under Roman Catholic law to poke their noses into anything they feel like. This includes investigations into grave delicts, or to use everyday language, violations of the law, such as acts which the Catholic Church considers as being the most serious of crimes. These "acts" include crimes against the Eucharist, crimes against the sanctity of the Sacrament of Penance, and most importantly, on this occasion and the sole reason Claudio Gabrielli had been summoned to the Holy

Father's office, crimes against the sixth commandment; "Thou shall not commit adultery". Signor Claudio Gabrielli did not have an official title as such and to most people outside of the Holy Office, he did not exist. If he were to be given an accurate title, it would be "Chief Inquisitor" or "Chief Enforcer of Doctrine", but no such role officially exists. To most people within the Vatican, he was simply known as the Head of the Holy Office. Claudio Gabrielli was Italian by birth coming from Palermo, the capital of Sicily, and it was here that he grew up surrounded by family members, most of whom were either in or had ties to the Cosa Nostra, or as most people called it – The Mafia. Signor Gabrielli had learnt his trade with the people he was surrounded by, and that knowledge meant he now had, at his disposal, an exhaustive and incredible list of ways in which he could make people submit to his will. He brought all that experience and knowledge with him, and to his role within the Holy Office. But countering that darker side of his make-up was the fact that despite everything, he had also been brought up a very strict Catholic. He now had a very healthy respect and deep love for the head of his church, and he knew that come what may, he would defend the Catholic faith, its doctrines and the wishes of the Holy Father, whatever they may be, until the day he died. This was the man Pope John XXIII had sent for. It took Claudio Gabrielli about ten minutes to walk from his office to the Pope's private quarters and he arrived breathless, but excited, to have been summoned.

Chapter Six
January 1961
The White House, Washington D.C.

The conversation with Father O'Boyle was not of any great importance, as far as Jack was concerned, as he had a country to run. He'd gotten off to a good start, and he'd received a lot of praise for his inaugural address, asking Americans to "ask not what your country can do for you, but what you can do for your country" and for the people of the world to "ask not what America will do for you, but what together we can do for the freedom of man". He was even congratulated on his speech by Soviet Premier Nikita Khrushchev. Earlier in the week, Jack had met with former President Harry S. Truman and he'd issued his first Executive Order, numbered 10914, directing a doubling of the quantity of surplus food distributed to needy families. He'd also nominated and hosted the swearing-in of his new cabinet. Jack's appointments included Defence Secretary Robert McNamara, Secretary of State Dean Rusk, and his National Security Advisor; a man named McGeorge Bundy. The CIA Directorship went to Allen Dulles and Chairman of the Joint Chiefs was Lyman Lemnitzer. Jack had also nominated Frank Burton Ellis for a federal judgeship on the United States District Court for the Eastern District of Louisiana. Not bad for a first week, he thought. Sitting alone in the Oval Office, Jack thought about where he was in life, what he'd already achieved and what laid before him. He had already experienced a number of family tragedies. His older brother, Joseph Junior, was killed in action in 1944 at the tender age of 29, when his plane exploded over the English Channel during a first attack execution of Operation Aphrodite during World War II. Then his younger sister, Rose Marie 'Rosemary' Kennedy, was born in 1918 with intellectual disabilities and underwent a prefrontal lobotomy at the age of 23, sadly leaving her permanently incapacitated. His other younger sister, Kathleen Agnes, had died in France as the result of a plane crash in 1948. On top of all that, his wife, Jacqueline Kennedy, had suffered a miscarriage in 1955 and a stillbirth in 1956: a daughter informally named Arabella and a son, Patrick Bouvier Kennedy, who died two days after his birth in August 1963. Jack thought back and realized the Pope possibly had a right to be worried. Sure, he had been single in the 1940s when he had affairs with Danish journalist Inga Arvad, the talented actress Gene Tierney and numerous others. But both before and even now, after he assumed the presidency, he was still having extramarital affairs with quite a number of women. The one thing that really concerned Jack was the public's reaction if these affairs became known. He was still thinking about this when Bobby entered the Oval.

'Morning, Jack,' he began. 'And how is the President feeling today?'

'Mmm,' he mused. 'I have been thinking about the Bishop's visit a couple of days ago and the Popes demands.'

'Aah, screw 'em, Jack. You're the President of the most powerful country in the world. Who you see and what you do in private is nobody's business but your own.'

'Yeah, I agree, Bobby, but I can't afford for any of this to become public and with this job and its demands, I don't have the time anymore to be setting up secret meetings with women. Even if I did, how the hell do I get to them without being seen?'

'It sounds to me like you need a new government department, Jack. How about having a word with Allen Dulles at the CIA? They're good at all that secrecy stuff.'

'Very funny, Bobby, no, it has to be kept in house,' replied Jack.

'You could always do something revolutionary, Jack; give up the women and try becoming a faithful husband,' said Bobby. 'Jackie's wonderful, and she's good for you.'

'I know that, and you know that I really do love Jackie, but this isn't a part-time hobby. It's like I've got a medical condition that means I need to have lots of women in my life.'

'OK,' said Bobby, 'but do you have to sleep with all of them?'

'That's kind of the point, Bobby,' he responded. 'Maybe I'm not the best husband and father in the world, but as I said, I do love Jackie and I love the kids. But despite that, I still have this need for having sex with other women. It's not something I feel I can control. It's like an addiction or even an illness. It's like having an itch that won't go away. The only relief I get is to scratch it, but then it damn well comes back again and I have to scratch it again.'

'So the question is, how we do we keep your itches and scratches secret and out of the press?' asked his younger brother. 'It's going to be one hell of a logistical problem, Jack, but I'll put some thought into it. You inspire affection and loyalty from the members of your team here at the White House, and your supporters all over the country, but I think we'll need to look outside the White House if this is going to work. I may need to put a team together of people who can be trusted one hundred percent to keep quiet. Oh, and whatever you do, don't let that creep J. Edgar get wind of any of this. Hoover can't be trusted, and I'm hoping that as United States Attorney General, I can clip his wings a bit.'

'Cheers, Bobby. Let me know how "Operation Scratch" pans out.'

.

Chapter Seven
January 1961
The Vatican, Rome, Italy

Signor Claudio Gabrielli now sat nervously in the private office of the Pope, with the Camerlengo to his right, seated in the chair beside him. He couldn't help but wonder what the "small problem" was that had brought him here.

'Signor Gabrielli, thank you for coming to see me so promptly,' began the Pope. 'As I mentioned to you on the telephone, I have a small problem which I would like you to deal with for me before it becomes a big problem.' The Pope reached into his desk and pulled out the same report in the buff-colored folder he had given to the Camerlengo to read a few days earlier. 'One of our Bishops has already tried a gentle approach through conversation, but it has been to no effect. Perhaps you would read through the report here and now, and then share with us any thoughts you may have on how to deal with the problem.'

'Of course, Holy Father,' said Gabrielli as he reached out and took the folder. He sat back in his chair, took the report out of its folder and started to read.

Report on the private life and extramarital activities of John Fitzgerald Kennedy.
Dated December 1960

Synopsis / Precis

The final conclusion of this report is undisputed by everyone involved in its compilation. There is no doubt whatsoever that John Fitzgerald Kennedy (hereinafter referred to as JFK), the President Elect of the United States of America, has frequent secret meetings, and numerous sexual relationships with women that he is not married to. There is a list of the women we have discovered further into this report, and there may well be, and probably are, many more that we, at this stage, know nothing about. It would appear that his wife, Jaqueline Kennedy, is aware of some, if not all, of these relationships, but she is, at this time, choosing to turn a blind eye for the sake of her marriage and her children. If this current state of affairs (please excuse the unintended pun) were to continue, and JFK does not stop his extramarital activities once he is in the White House, then we can see no way in which these affairs and his extramarital activities would not become public. As he is the first Roman Catholic President of the United States, the Catholic world in America would look to their President as well as to the Holy Father in setting the moral standards that all Catholics should aim for and abide by. The world is changing extremely fast, and with the advent of live television, the possible disclosure of a secret affair would soon become very public knowledge, and would be reported in newspapers, magazines, radio and television everywhere in America. It is our view that the same information and gory detail could, and in our considered view, undoubtedly would, be broadcast around the world before there is time to stop or prevent it. It is, therefore, this report's recommendation that in order to prevent Roman Catholics the world over taking the view that "what is perfectly OK and good enough for the President of the United States, must be perfectly OK and good enough for the rest of us" then the illicit affairs of JFK must be stopped at all costs. Detailed report continues below.

Gabrielli looked up from the report. 'I have read through the initial synopsis, Holy Father, and I now fully understand what you referred to as your small problem. Should I read the full report now, or should I take it with me and read the detail later?'

'Please take it with you. That is a copy and I have the original safely locked away in my private safe. Myself, the Camerlengo and the Bishop I asked to speak to the President are the only three people that are aware of the situation. Plus, now, of course, yourself. I would like to keep it that way.'

'Of course, Holy Father,' said Gabrielli.

'If it were to become public knowledge,' said the Camerlengo, 'that the church had not been able to prevent the world's most prominent member of the Catholic faith from committing adultery on a regular basis, then the church would lose all of its credibility. The people would see adultery as completely acceptable behavior, quickly followed, no doubt, by the regular use of contraception and uncontrolled abortions worldwide.'

'Do you have any suggestions, Signor Gabrielli?' asked the Pope.

'Of course,' said Gabrielli, smiling. 'Back in my home town of Palermo, we would simply ask one of the brethren to eliminate the problem.'

'I fear that is not an option we would care to consider,' said the Camerlengo, returning Claudio Gabrielli's smile. He then smiled as he looked across at the Pope for confirmation of his opinion, but the Holy Father simply stared back at him. Cardinal Masella couldn't work out what the stare and the silence signified, if anything

'If the President will not listen to you, Holy Father,' said Gabrielli, 'perhaps the ladies he is consorting with might be open to persuasion.'

'I fear none of them are ladies as we would understand the term,' commented the Pope. 'But please don't let that stop you trying. Please take the report with you, Signor, read it thoroughly, and when you are ready with a plan of action, make an appointment through the Camerlengo here to come and see me again.'

Gabrielli stood and, taking the Holy Father's hand, kissed the back of it. 'I shall give the matter all my attention,' he said.

'I would hope so,' said Pope John, and with that, Gabrielli left the office, closing the heavy wooden door behind him.

'You worried me for a moment there, Angelo,' said Camerlengo Masella, 'when Signor Gabrielli mentioned his Mafia past, and one of the brethren eliminating the problem, both he and I smiled at the ridiculous prospect, but you, however, did not.'

'Let me ask you an extremely important question, my good friend,' said the Pope, putting his hands together with all his fingers pointing upwards and his elbows firmly planted on the surface of the desk 'Please think very carefully before you answer me, and be totally honest with your reply. Which of these two options would you regard as being the more important; the entire future of the Holy Catholic faith worldwide, or the incredibly decadent and totally immoral life of one sinful man?'

The Camerlengo looked thoughtfully at Pope John XXIII, but decided to say nothing.

Chapter Eight
January 1961
The Palace of the Holy Office
Just Outside Vatican City

Claudio Gabrielli could not be happier. The Pope himself had just entrusted him with a highly secret and holy mission, to protect the name and reputation of the church. He would, of course, ensure that, as the Pope had insisted, nobody else knew the full picture or let even one word slip out, but he knew straight away that he could not do this on his own. He needed a team. A team that he could trust implicitly to do whatever it was that was needed, and to keep their mouths shut, even under the most severe torture (not that he would ever let it come to that). He pulled an exercise-sized book with a hard maroon cover out of the center drawer of his large teak-colored desk. The drawer was kept locked at all times, and he had the only key to it on a strong chain from his belted waistband into his left-hand trouser pocket. In the book, of which this was the only copy, were the details of every member of the staff of the "Supreme Sacred Congregation of the Holy Office" (although he still much preferred the original title of "The Inquisition"). The details he had collated over the years gave him an intimate knowledge of everyone working in the Palace of the Holy Office. Of course, a lot of the staff in his book were simply secretarial or ladies that cleaned and made tea and coffee. But also in the book were the names and details of people he knew he could count on as operatives. People who he trusted implicitly, and who would not be afraid to go anywhere or do whatever it was he deemed necessary to meet his objective. He had worked out in his mind that he needed to put together a team of five, including himself. Each member would need to be a specialist, and it had to be an all-male team. The last thing he needed was jealousy in the team if he brought a woman along and besides, he didn't really like women anyway. Gabrielli had brought two people with him from his old life in Palermo, and they would do his bidding without asking any difficult questions. Even though they were not devout Catholics like him, they had a sort of faith, and that was good enough for Signor Gabrielli. After an hour of going through his book, he finalized the team. The first name on his list, and always his second-in-command, was Mario Orsini. Mario was, like himself, born and brought up inside a Sicilian Mafia family, and he learnt there what family was all about. His family now lived here in Rome at the Palace of the Holy Office. Mario Orsini's specialist skill was that of not-so-gentle persuasion, or as the popular press called it – torture. Claudio Gabrielli never used that word, and he would never sanction the use of torture if it could possibly be avoided, but you never knew how things were going to turn out, and it was always good to have the option there if needed.

Marco Farina was the exact opposite to Mario. Marco, also from Palermo and the second man Gabrielli had brought with him, was what most people would describe as a true ladies' man, and he seemed to be able to talk any women into his bed within five minutes of meeting them. Gabrielli felt it was important to have Marco on the team as they were mostly going to be dealing with women. Marco Farina, with his sultry good looks, boyish charms coupled with a silvery tongue, and a physique truly sent from the gods, seemed the obvious choice. Giuseppe Mancuso was his technical expert. If they needed to break in somewhere, or to be able to listen in to phone calls, then Giuseppe was the man for the job. His parents were both Italian, but Giuseppe himself had been born and brought up in America; New York to be exact. After school, he'd trained as a telephone engineer and was a natural at all the technical aspects. But he found it boring. At the age of 26, he decided to return to Italy; to Rome in particular (the home of his father). He got a part-time job with the telephone company in Rome, which left him plenty of spare time to supplement his income with other casual jobs, or just use the time to relax in some of Rome's bars and nightclubs. He met Claudio Gabrielli in one such bar one evening and they got chatting. Before he knew it, Giuseppe had got a job working with, but not for the Holy Office. Gabrielli only called upon him when he had a technical problem coming up. That was six years ago, and Giuseppe was about to receive another phone call requiring the use of his specialist skills. A very useful aspect of having Giuseppe on the team was that he spoke his English with an American accent, and on this new job for the Pope, that skill might prove to be very helpful. Lastly, there was Franco Lamberti. Franco was from a small town in Lombardy called Soriano nel Cimino, and his skill; Franco could shoot the pips out of an apple from 800 feet away, and there was nothing he didn't know about guns, rifles and weaponry. So, that was the team, and two hours later, Gabrielli telephoned the Camerlengo and asked for a second meeting with the Holy Father in order to outline his ideas.

Chapter Nine
January 1961
The Vatican, Rome, Italy

'So, that is my plan Holy Father,' said Gabrielli 'Three simple steps. We always try step one first, but if it doesn't work, we then have to move on to step two. If that doesn't work either, then we will make all the necessary preparations for step three, but we do not action step three without your confirmed go ahead.'

'That all sounds excellent, Signor Gabrielli, and all I can do is wish you and your team undoubted success,' responded Pope John. 'Please keep me personally informed on my private line. Please don't bother the Camerlengo with any of this, I will ensure he is informed of everything.'

At 10.00 am sharp, Gabrielli left the Vatican, and two hours later, having telephoned both Giuseppe and Franco, he collected the three Rome-based members of his team. They and their suitcases all headed for Rome's airport, where they met up with Franco who had gotten a train into Rome. Three hours later, all five of them flew to Washington D.C. The Camerlengo arrived at the Pope's private office at 4.00 pm; the time he'd agreed earlier with the Pope, but 40 minutes after Claudio Gabrielli had departed for the USA.

'I am so sorry about this, Benedetto,' began the Pope, 'but it could not be helped. The timing of my meeting with Signor Gabrielli had to be changed. I tried to get hold of you but without success, so I am afraid we went ahead with the meeting without you. You haven't really missed much to be honest, he has a very simple two-stage plan, and he said he will keep us informed at every stage as he proceeds.'

The Camerlengo nodded.

Well, thought the Pope, what the Camerlengo doesn't know can't hurt him.

Chapter Ten
February 1961
The White House, Washington D.C.

Jack was relieved. His "State of the Union" address to the joint session of the United States Congress had gone down much better than he had anticipated. Now, on the first day of a new month, he was about to hold his second presidential news conference. Sitting at his desk in the Oval Office he flicked through the pages of his desk diary. Evelyn ran a very tight ship when it came to his appointments, but he liked to have a reference of his own. Later in the day, he would be holding his first meeting of the National Security Council, to be followed by sending a letter to Defence Secretary McNamara about the scheduled launch of the USS Sam Houston the following day. He turned the page again and found another full day of activities. First, a meeting with NATO's Supreme Allied Commander and another with the Joint Chiefs Chairman. Mentally putting work to one side, Jack sat there thinking about an old English saying he'd learnt as a child, which now seemed extremely appropriate – "All work and no play makes Jack a very dull boy". When was he going to find time to "scratch his itch", as he now referred to it? He must find out how Bobby was progressing in getting him some secret "scratching time".

Chapter Eleven
February 1961
The Willard Hotel, Washington D.C.

Claudio Gabrielli and his team had checked into two twin rooms and a suite for himself at the Willard Hotel, just two blocks from the White House. A hotel had been on this site since 1816, but it wasn't until Henry and Edwin Willard purchased the property in 1850 that it first gained fame. President Zachary Taylor stayed at the hotel soon after it opened, and Abraham Lincoln, amid assassination threats, covertly checked in and stayed for the 10 days leading up to his inauguration. Ulysses S. Grant often relaxed with brandy and a cigar in the hotel's lobby, and the story goes that he was frequently approached by political operatives pushing and promoting various causes whom he later nicknamed "lobbyists". The term stuck and is still used to this day. Stage one of Gabrielli's plan was very simple. Find the women Kennedy is involved with, and have a gentle word in their ear, along the lines of "don't go near the President again or you could end up six feet under". Not very subtle or original he admitted, but it was usually very effective. He knew from the Pope's report who most of the women were, but the question was where he could find them. Gabrielli decided to simply start at the top of the list of names and work his way down. The first name in the report was that of Inga Arvad, with whom JFK had had an affair during World War II. 'The JFK Report' as its plain front cover called it, stated that throughout the war, the FBI had Inga Arvad under constant surveillance because they believed she might be a German spy. She was, in fact, no more than an extremely talented Danish journalist, but she had come under suspicion for being the personal guest of the German Leader Adolf Hitler at the 1936 Summer Olympics. Her affair with JFK had been back in 1941 and 1942, and having been born in 1913, and it now being 1961, that would make her 47 years old. Gabrielli decided she was no longer a threat. The second name on his list was that of a young Swedish woman named Gunilla von Post. This certainly looked far more promising, he thought, as he read the details. According to the report, she and Kennedy had met by chance on the French Riviera in August 1953. The young Swede was only 21 at the time and JFK was 36. She had been sent there by her aristocrat father to brush up on her French. Kennedy, it appeared, had been immediately blown away by her natural blonde beauty. She would only be 29 now, and from what he'd read about JFK, they were probably still meeting regularly. She was certainly worth a visit anyway. Gabrielli walked out of his hotel room and walked straight into the room next door without knocking.

'Mario, round up the boys and meet me in the lobby. We are all going to do a house call on a young lady who can probably help us.'

They had hired a large car, a Lincoln, and Franco drove them to the home of Gunilla von Post. Gabrielli did not want anyone to see the car parked outside von Post's house and perhaps report it later to the police, so they parked on a side street and walked.

'Stay in the car, boys, but keep an eye open, and if necessary, keep everyone away from the house. I don't want to be disturbed. Come on, Mario, you're with me.' The two of them got out of the car, turned right onto the correct street, walked about fifty yards and then, opening the gate, walked up the driveway and knocked on her front door. They were in luck; Gunilla von Post was at home, and not only that, she was home alone. Gabrielli spun her a line about reports of possible subsidence in the area and they had come to warn her and have a quick look round the house for any signs of cracks. It was all just a ruse, of course, to get them inside the house, but Gunilla von Post didn't know that, and she let them both in.

'I'm sorry we deceived you at the door, Miss von Post,' began Gabrielli, 'but we need to talk to you about your relationship with President Kennedy.'

She looked slightly taken aback, but she remained calm and simply sat in an armchair. She waved her hand at the two others, indicating her visitors should be seated as well.

'So, how can I help you, gentlemen?' she asked.

'We need to know about your relationship, how it started and is it still going on,' replied Gabrielli. 'Assuming you cooperate, no harm will come to you or anybody else, and you can forget this conversation ever happened.'

Gunilla was obviously shocked by the not-so-vague implied threats, but she chose to rise above them and answer as best she could. What alternative did she have? 'The President and I met purely by chance,' she began, 'while I was visiting the French Riviera, and that was way back in August 1953. He was a totally charming and, at the time, quite boyish-looking 36-year-old senator from Massachusetts. I was just 21, and I had been sent to the Cote d'Azur by my father for a month to try and improve my French language skills.'

'Did you start your affair that night?' asked Gabrielli.

'Certainly not,' she replied, deeply offended, it appeared. 'We simply spent a very pleasant evening together. Dinner, dancing, and a moonlit walk to the shore of the Mediterranean. At one point, he turned and kissed me tenderly and, to be honest, my breath was taken away. Please understand, I was just 21 years old at the time, the daughter of a Swedish aristocrat, alone in a foreign country and this was all new to me. At one point, he broke the silence and softly said, 'I fell in love with you tonight.'

'So, you started your affair straight after that?' he asked again.

'Again, no. Jack admitted there and then that there was a big problem for us being together as he was about to get married. He then said, 'If only I had met you one week before,

I would have cancelled the whole thing.' I'm not sure if he would have, but I like to think he meant it at the time.'

'So, what happened after that?' Gabrielli asked. This was taking forever!

'Oh, Jack returned to America where, three weeks later, on September 1st, 1953, he married Jacqueline Bouvier. But being honest with you, despite him now being married, I was still totally smitten with him, and I was thrilled when I received the first of a series of love letters. Plus, I received several trans-Atlantic phone calls in between the letters, and Jack spoke of his hopes of organizing what he described as a clandestine reunion.'

'And did that happen?'

'Yes, it did. Our relationship was finally consummated, which I believe is the polite expression, when Jack contrived to visit Sweden with a friend in August 1955. I was relatively inexperienced, and Jack's tenderness was a revelation.'

'I don't need all the gory details, Miss von Post,' he interrupted.

''Well,' Jack said, 'We've waited two years for this, it seems almost too good to be true, and I want to make you happy.' We made love time and time again and spent a glorious week together. I even introduced Jack to some of my family and friends.'

'So, Miss. The most important question, and please be honest with us. Is it still going on, and are you still having an affair with the President?'

'Good heavens, no. Our week together ended with some painful farewells at the airport, and although the night before Jack repeatedly told me he loved me and that he'd do everything he could to be with me, I knew it would never happen.'

'And that's the last you saw of him? Honestly?'

'Yes, I knew it could go nowhere. One evening, while he was with me, Jack called his father Joe to tell him he wanted to divorce Jackie and marry me. But his father was having none of it, telling him divorce was completely out of the question because it would ruin Jack's hopes of making it to the White House. I knew then that it was over.'

'Have you ever heard from him since?' Gabrielli asked her.

'Oh yes,' she replied. 'Jack made several attempts to persuade me to move to the USA. He suggested New York and said he could help me get work as a model, but I told him I refused to accept anything short of marriage. Look, basically, I borrowed him from his wife for a week. For me, it was a beautiful week that no one can ever take away from me. But that was, and is, the end of it, even though I now live in the USA, I have no contact with him.' Gabrielli stood up and Mario followed his lead.

'Thank you for your candor, Miss van Post. We shan't be bothering you again, but please don't mention our little chat to anyone, otherwise we may have to return. Goodbye.' And with that, the two men walked out the door, shutting it behind them.

Chapter Twelve
March 1961
The White House, Washington D.C.

On June the 17th, 1950, Bobby Kennedy had married socialite Ethel Skakel, the third daughter of businessman George and Ann Skakel, at St. Mary's Catholic Church in Greenwich, Connecticut. By March 1961, the couple had 7 children; Kathleen who was born in 1951, Joseph who was born in 1952, Robert Junior who was born in 1954, David who was born in 1955, Courtney who was born in 1956, Michael who was born in 1958 and Kerry who was born in 1959. Bobby and Ethel eventually had 11 children, and it was safe to say, Bobby was very much a family man.

Bobby owned a home at the well-known Kennedy compound on Cape Cod, in Hyannis Port, Massachusetts, but he spent most of his time at his estate in McLean, Virginia, known as Hickory Hill, which was located west of Washington, D.C.

Bobby was said by everyone that knew the family to be the gentlest and shyest of the boys, as well as being the least articulate orally. By the time he was a young boy, his grandmother, Josie Fitzgerald, worried he would become what she described as a sissy. His mother had a similar concern as he was the smallest and the thinnest, but soon afterward, the family discovered there was no fear of that. Family friend Lem Billings met Bobby when he was just 8 years old and would later reflect that he loved him, adding that Bobby Kennedy was the nicest little boy he'd ever met. Billings also said that Bobby was barely noticed in the early days, but that's because he didn't bother anyone. Luella

Hennessey, who became the nurse for the Kennedy children when Bobby was 12, called him the most thoughtful and considerate of all his siblings.

Bobby was certainly teased by his siblings, as in their family it was the norm for humor to be displayed in that fashion. He would often turn jokes on himself or remain silent. Despite his gentle demeanor, he could still be outspoken, and Bobby once engaged a priest in a public argument that horrified his mother, but she later conceded that he had been correct all along. Even when arguing for a noble cause, his comments could have a cutting quality.

Although Joe Kennedy's most ambitious dreams centered on his older brothers, Bobby maintained the code of personal loyalty that seemed to infuse the life of his family. His competitiveness was admired by his father and his elder brothers, while his loyalty bound them more affectionately close.

Being a rather timid child, Bobby was often the target of his father's very dominating temperament. But working on the campaigns of older brother Jack, he became more and more involved, passionate, and tenacious than the candidate himself. Bobby was obsessed with detail, fighting every battle, and taking workers to task. He had always been far closer to Jack than any of the other members of the family.

Bobby's opponents on Capitol Hill maintained that his collegiate magnanimity was sometimes hindered by a tenacious and somewhat impatient manner. His professional life was dominated by the same attitudes that governed his family life: a certainty that good humor and leisure must be balanced by service and accomplishment. Bobby Kennedy could be both the most ruthlessly diligent and yet, at the same time, generously adaptable of politicians, at once both temperamental and forgiving. In this, he was very much his father's son, lacking truly lasting emotional independence, and yet possessing a great desire to contribute. He lacked the innate self-confidence of his contemporaries, yet he found great self-assurance in the experience of married life; an experience that he stated had given him a base of self-belief in the public arena.

Upon hearing yet again the assertion that he was ruthless, Bobby once joked to a reporter, 'If I find out who has called me ruthless I will destroy him.' He also confessed to possessing a bad temper that required self-control: 'My biggest problem,' he said, 'as counsel is to keep my temper. I think we all feel that when a witness comes before the United States Senate, he has an obligation to speak frankly and tell the truth. To see people sit in front of us and lie and evade makes me boil inside. But you can't lose your temper; if you do, the witness has gotten the best of you.'

In his earlier life, Bobby Kennedy had developed a reputation as the family's attack dog. He was a hostile cross-examiner on Joseph McCarthy's Senate committee, a fixer and leg-breaker as JFK's campaign manager, an unforgiving and merciless cutthroat; his father's son right down to Joseph Kennedy's purported observation that "he hates like me". Yet, Bobby Kennedy somehow became a liberal icon and an anti-war visionary. Bobby had inherited his faith from his family, and it is fair to say he was more religious than all of his brothers and approached all his duties with a very Catholic view of the world.

This was the dilemma Bobby now faced at this particular time in his life. He didn't like his older brother's attitude to his private life one little bit; the way he treated Jackie and his constant affairs with numerous different women. But nevertheless, Bobby loved Jack dearly and despite everything, he would do anything he could for his older brother.

Jack was seated at his desk in the Oval Office when Bobby entered. He motioned to his older brother that he should leave the desk and come over and join him on the sofa, indicating with a raised index finger to his lips that they should speak quietly.

'I've made some progress regarding 'Operation Scratch.''

'Fantastic,' said the President, keeping his voice almost to a whisper. 'I've put together a team of four guys who can be trusted one hundred percent. They know what this is all about, and they have no problem with it. They're all single so have no wives to blab to, and they understand they can never say anything to anyone.'

'So, how is this going to work,' asked Jack.

'Evelyn controls your diary, but she should never know about any of this.'

'Oh come on, Bobby, Evelyn has been with me so many years now that I'm pretty sure she knows I'm not the most faithful husband the world has ever known.'

'Maybe, Jack, but she can't know details.'

'Fair enough,' replied the President. 'We need to come up with some committee that sounds perfectly legit to Evelyn, but you and I both know you won't be doing much talking at the committee meetings, and there won't be any minutes recorded.'

'How often can the committee meet?' asked Jack.

'If you don't want to arouse too much suspicion, Jack, I would suggest a maximum of two committee meetings a week. Make sure they don't clash with anything important in the official diary, and in the meantime, I'll get one of the guys on the team to rent a small house somewhere private where you can hold your committee meetings. I'll get one of them to pick up the committee members and drive them home after the meetings.'

'Sounds brilliant, Bobby. How soon is the first committee meeting?'

'Just hold fire for another couple of days, Jack, while I sort out the house and a couple of vehicles. I'll get back to you as soon as I can.'

'I suppose I better get back to the day job then,' said Jack.

'Anything interesting coming up?' asked his brother.

'To be honest, no, not a lot. Oh, I've decided to sign a commission restoring the Five Star General Rank of the Army, and I'm awarding it to former President Eisenhower.'

'Great idea, Jack. He'll love that.'

Bobby left the Oval office and set off to finalize details for Operation Scratch, and Jack went back to his paperwork, muttering to himself, 'Nothing exciting ever really happens in this job.'

Chapter Thirteen
April 12th, 1961
The White House, Washington D.C.

Bobby burst into the Oval Office unannounced.

'Turn the TV on, Jack, you need to see this.'

The Presenter was repeating what had been said just a few minutes earlier.

'It is being reported from Moscow that the Soviet Union has successfully carried out the first manned spaceflight in history. The spacecraft, which is named Vostok 1, was launched from Baikonur Cosmodrome this morning, April 12th 1961, with Soviet cosmonaut Yuri Gagarin aboard, making him the first human to cross into outer space.'

'Oh bloody hell,' fumed Jack, watching the TV.

The TV presenter continued.

'Details of the flight have been issued by Moscow, and they tell us that the orbital spaceflight consisted of a single orbit around Earth which skimmed the upper atmosphere at 91 nautical miles at its lowest point. The flight took just 108 minutes from launch to landing. Gagarin parachuted to the ground separately from his capsule after ejecting at an altitude of 23,000 feet.'

'Turn it off, Bobby,' Jack commanded. 'That's all I need; the bloody Soviets telling the world how superior they are to the United States.'

'You better telephone Khrushchev and congratulate him,' said Bobby.

'Really,' queried Jack.

'Of course you must. Come on, Jack, you don't want to look like a sore loser.'

'No, you're right.'

'Offer him something like "congratulations to the Soviet Union for your outstanding technical achievement".'

'God, Bobby, you ought to be sitting in this chair, not me. You're far better at this sort of stuff than I am. I'd rather just tell him we'll do something to put his little trip round the planet to shame. I don't know, something like, 'the U.S. will land a man on the moon before the decade is out. So up yours Nikita Sergeyevich Khrushchev.'

'Yeah, great idea, Jack, but for the time being, just say well done.'

Jack picked up the phone and Evelyn answered immediately. 'Evelyn, can you try and get Khrushchev on the phone for me please?'

'Can you repeat that please, Mr. President?'

'Certainly, Evelyn. Can you please try and get me through on the telephone to speak with Nikita Sergeyevich Khrushchev, First Secretary of the Communist Party of the Soviet Union? You must have heard of him, Evelyn. He's a short chubby chap with a bald head. Wears terrible ill-fitting suits.'

Evelyn was laughing on the other end of the phone.

'Oh, and I guess you better send in a Russian interpreter to be on the extension. Thank you, Evelyn.'

'My pleasure, Mr. President,' she replied, still giggling.

'Good grief, Jack,' said Bobby, 'you give that poor woman such a hard time. What the hell would you, or the White House for that matter, do without her?'

'Oh I know that, Bobby. She's totally irreplaceable.'

'Well, it might be a nice idea to tell her that occasionally,' said his brother.

At that point, the door to the Oval Office opened and Evelyn entered saying, 'I have a Viktor Sukhodrev, First Secretary Khrushchev's interpreter on the telephone for you Mr. President. Shall I put him through?'

Jack looked across the Oval Office at Bobby who was still seated on one of the sofas. His younger brother nodded his head, and Jack shrugged his shoulders and answered, 'Yes please, Evelyn, and thank you. I don't know what I'd do without you.'

'I do, Mr. President,' she replied, 'but I'd rather not say.' This time, both Jack and Bobby laughed. Evelyn returned to her desk, and immediately the phone on his desk rang.

Jack picked it up, and on the other end, a voice speaking perfect English said, 'Good morning, Mr. President. My name is Viktor Sukhodrev and I am First Secretary Khrushchev's interpreter. He is alongside me as we speak, and I will tell him word-for-word whatever it is you wish to say.'

'Thank you, Mr. Sukhodrev. Would you please tell First Secretary Khrushchev that I would like, on behalf of the United States of America, to congratulate the Soviet Union for your outstanding technical achievement.'

Jack could hear the interpreter on the other end relaying his message in Russian. 'The First Secretary thanks you, Mr. President, and he is pleased that you have recognized the Soviet Union's great triumph of science and technology, once more demonstrating the superiority of the socialist system over that of capitalism.'

'Well, I'm not sure I can agree with that sentiment, but nevertheless, I once again congratulate the Soviet Union on its achievement. Goodbye, Mr. Sukhodrev.' The President replaced the telephone in its cradle. 'That bloody man drives me insane.' Jack fumed. 'Did you hear that rubbish? 'Once more demonstrating the superiority of the socialist system over that of capitalism.' I may have been joking earlier, Bobby, but I tell you this, in the not too distant future, I'm going to announce to the world that the United States of America will win this "space race" by putting a man on the moon before the end of the decade.'

'Don't you think we ought to check if it's possible before you say something?'

'Aah, cobblers to that, Bobby. I'm sure we can, but if we can't then we'll fake it. Let's face it, there's nobody up there to report back that we never arrived, so we'll just tell everyone we did, even if we didn't. Who the hell's going to know the difference?'

'The astronauts might!' replied Bobby.

'Yes, well. Oh, I don't know, bro; look we can pay them off or make them overseas ambassadors or something they want. I'm sure it will work if we need to. But seriously, Bobby,' retorted Jack, 'I really do believe there's nothing this country can't do if it puts its mind to it. We've got the best scientific brains in the world here in the States and I'm sure we can put a man on the moon.'

'And bring him back alive?' asked Bobby.

'Yeah, that too, I hope,' smiled Jack.

Chapter Fourteen
April 14th, 1961
The Vatican, Rome, Italy

Pope John XXIII was in his private quarters, stretched out on his massive double bed. He had been dozing off in the chair and decided a short rest was what was needed. He was not a young man anymore and he found he got tired quite quickly. There was a knock on his bedroom door, and he knew it had to be the Camerlengo. Nobody else had access to his personal quarters.

'Come in, Benedetto,' he said, and propped himself up on top of the bed.

'I am sorry to disturb you, Angelo, but I was worried when I found you missing from your desk at this hour of the day. Are you OK?'

'Oh, I'm fine,' he replied. 'I just get a little tired in the afternoons, and I think I will, whenever possible, follow the example of our southern European neighbor's, and perhaps start having a little afternoon siesta.'

'Well, it will, of course, be possible whenever you say it is possible. Nobody is going to contradict the Pope if he decides to take a rest in the afternoons. You are approaching your 80th birthday my friend, and a little tiredness is to be expected.'

'You are two years older than me, Benedetto, so don't you start lecturing me on the need for rest.'

'Ah, I may be older, Angelo, but I do not carry the full weight and responsibility of the largest church in the world on my shoulders as you have to.'

'Yes, and I have to say, at times it feels exceedingly heavy,' the Pope replied.

'Any news from Signor Claudio Gabrielli,' asked the Camerlengo. 'He has been in the United States for some time now, and I assume he is working on the small problem?'

'I heard from him yesterday. He has so far contacted eleven different women whom the President has had affairs with, but he has assured me that in every case, they have ended. He is also convinced that Mrs. Kennedy is fully aware of her husband's extramarital relationships, but she is not prepared to do anything to "rock the boat" as they say, while he is still President.'

'So what is Gabrielli doing next?' asked the Camerlengo.

'He is going to see a woman named…' the Pope leaned over on the bed and pulled out a sheet of paper from the top drawer of his bedside cabinet. 'Ah, yes. A woman named Mary Pinchot Meyer. Gabrielli has no definite proof yet, but he is fairly certain she is still secretly meeting with President Kennedy.'

Chapter Fifteen
April 14th, 1961
The White House, Washington D.C.

'What the hell do we do about Cuba?' asked Jack.

Seated with him in the Oval Office were the six men whom he relied on for advice in numerous areas of government. Defence Secretary Robert McNamara, who never held back in letting Jack know his opinion, and Secretary of State Dean Rusk also spoke up whenever he had something to say. National Security Advisor McGeorge Bundy was a different personality entirely and he never offered an opinion unless Jack asked him to. It wasn't that he didn't have opinions; it was just the way he preferred to work. Jack had also asked CIA Director Allen Dulles to attend the meeting along with the Chairman of the Joint Chiefs Lyman Lemnitzer and Bobby in his role as U.S. Attorney General.

'I think, perhaps, a better, or should I say, more appropriate question, Mr. President, is; what the hell do we do about Fidel Castro?' said Allen Dulles.

'OK, agreed,' said Jack. 'But does the CIA have an answer?'

'Possibly, Mr. President,' answered Dulles. 'As you know, Sir, after the Cuban Revolution in 1959, Castro began forging strong economic links with the Soviet Union. Your predecessor, President Dwight D. Eisenhower, was extremely concerned at the direction Castro's government was taking at the time, and so, in March 1960, President Eisenhower allocated $13.1 million to the CIA with the specific aim of planning Castro's overthrow. However, Eisenhower's term of office was coming to an end, and he thought it was more prudent to leave the final decision as to trying to overthrow Castro or not to the incoming President.'

'And this plan still exists and could be implemented?' queried Jack.

'Yes, Mr. President.'

'Give us the basic details, Director,' Jack commanded Dulles. The CIA Director reached over and pulled a file from his briefcase.

'The plan is, in one sense, very simple. But in another way, it is quite complex. Basically, we invade Cuba.'

'I'm sorry, Allen,' interrupted Robert McNamara, the Defence Secretary. 'I could not possibly authorize or recommend U.S. forces invading Cuba. It is unthinkable.'

'That's not the plan, Robert,' Dulles replied. 'Our plan involves using a counter revolutionary military group, made up of mostly Cuban exiles who fled here to the United States after Castro's takeover, but also some seconded U.S. military personnel, trained and funded by the CIA. They are known as Brigade 2506 and they are fronted by the armed wing of the Democratic Revolutionary Front. Nobody would be in United States uniforms or have any military tags hanging round their necks. Nothing could ever be traced back to the United States.'

'And where does this army of yours leave from and where do they land?' asked Lyman Lemnitzer, Chairman of the Joint Chiefs.

'Over 1,400 paramilitaries, divided into five infantry battalions and one paratrooper battalion, will be assembled in Guatemala before setting out for Cuba by boat. Then two days later, eight CIA-supplied B-26 bombers will attack Cuban airfields and then return to the U.S. The following night, the main invasion force will land at a beach named Playa Girón in an area known as the Bay of Pigs.'

'Chances of success, Allen?' asked Jack.

'The CIA would estimate at least 85%,' replied the CIA Director.

'In that case, do it,' commanded Jack.

Chapter Sixteen
April 21st, 1961
The White House, Washington D.C.

'What a prize balls up, Allen,' said Jack. 'Tell me in words of one syllable, what the hell happened to your 85% chance of success? The United States now looks totally incompetent. Your invading force was defeated within three days by the Cuban Revolutionary Armed Forces, and to make matters worse, they were under the direct command of Castro.'

'I'm sorry, Mr. President, but the original plan we devised required both air and naval support, but we got neither. As a result, the operation only had half the forces the CIA plan had deemed necessary. It started well enough and we were in control, having initially overwhelmed a local revolutionary militia. While the Cuban Army's counter-offensive was led by José Ramón Fernández, and while he was running things, we were well on top. But then Castro decided to take personal control of the operation.'

'So you're telling me Castro is a military genius and that's why the invaders surrendered after only three days, with the majority being publicly interrogated and put into Cuban prisons?'

'No, Mr. President. The critical factor in this was, as I said before, the lack of air and naval support. If we had received that, we would have in all probability succeeded.'

'Well, I have to tell you, Allen,' began Jack. 'This failed invasion of yours has helped to strengthen the position of Castro's leadership, and it's made him a bloody national hero. Even worse, it has also strengthened the relations between Cuba and the Soviet Union and that, I definitely don't like. I suggest you leave me in peace, Allen, before I say or do something I will later regret.'

As Allen Dulles left the Oval Office with his tail between his legs, Bobby came in.

'God Bobby, this administration has been severely embarrassed, and at the moment, I could quite happily splinter the CIA into a thousand pieces and scatter it into the wind.'

'Don't do anything in haste, Jack,' said Bobby, always playing the peacemaker. 'Allen Dulles is basically a good man and he's very sound. He's the right man to head-up the CIA at the moment, and what's more, he daren't screw up again. After this cockup, you've got him well and truly by the balls. So use it.'

Chapter Seventeen
May 1961
Washington D.C., United States

Mary Eno Pinchot Meyer was an American artist and painter who lived in Washington D.C. She had been married to CIA official Cord Meyer from 1945 to 1958, and according to the report Gabrielli held in his hand, she and President Kennedy had, and probably still were seeing each other after her marriage to Meyer ended. The report stated that Mary Meyer visited the President frequently at the White House and was known by several unnamed sources to be one of his many mistresses. That was enough for Gabrielli, and so they decided to pay Mary Eno Pinchot Meyer a visit. Gabrielli thought he would take all four of his assistants to see Mary Meyer as he felt a simple show of force would hopefully be enough to deter her. They knocked on her front door, and as she opened it, Franco and Mario pushed straight past her and stood behind her. She was now surrounded front and back.

'May we come in, Mrs. Meyer?' asked Gabrielli.

'Who are you and what do you want?' she demanded. 'I've got nothing in the house worth stealing.'

'I think we'll all come in anyway,' said Gabrielli, and he too pushed past her. Marco came after him, Giuseppe came in last and closed the front door behind him. They all sat on various chairs in the lounge and Mary Meyer sat down as well, feeling she had no choice. She was one lone, defenseless woman against five men. Gabrielli's tactics were already working. 'I want to have a nice little informal chat with you about your relationship with a certain Mr. John Fitzgerald Kennedy who, as you know, now happens to be the President

71

of the United States. I don't care what you've done in the past, but I tell you now, it stops immediately.'

'What Jack and I do in private is nothing to do with anybody else.'

'Oh, I think it is,' said Gabrielli in a very soft, gentle tone. He'd always found a soft gentle voice was far more intimidating than shouting at someone, especially when it came to dealing with women.

'If she's going to be awkward boss,' said Mario, 'do you want me to pull her fingernails out? I always enjoy doing that.'

'No, not at the moment. I think Mrs. Meyer will agree to our wishes without resorting to violence at this stage, although that could, of course, change.'

'What do you want of me?' she repeated.

'You obviously weren't paying attention, lady,' said Mario. 'Shall I spell it out for you? Stop your affair with Kennedy now. Today. Not tomorrow or perhaps next week sometime. Now. Understood?'

'And what happens if I don't? All I have to do is tell him I'm being threatened and he'll have you all killed.'

'Oh dear,' said Gabrielli, faking a worried look. 'We better change our minds then, lads, and leave this poor lady alone to make her phone call to her lover.'

'Might be a bit difficult making a phone call boss if she's dead,' said Franco, pulling a revolver out from under his jacket and loudly spinning the chamber for effect.

'You won't kill me,' she said, trying to appear strong and not worried, although in reality she was now petrified, even though she was trying not to show it.

'Let me explain the situation to you one last time,' said Gabrielli. 'The choice is yours, and the choice is extremely simple. You stop seeing Kennedy and you live. You continue to see him, and you die. I don't think I can make it any clearer than that.'

'Got it, lady?' asked Mario.

'Yes, I think I've got it now, thank you,' she replied with tremor in her voice.

'We're going to leave you now,' said Gabrielli, 'but we will be watching you. Go to Kennedy even once more and you will come to a speedy and untimely end. My good friend here,' he said, pointing at Franco, 'is an unbelievably brilliant shot, and he would quite happily, without any hesitation at all, put a bullet in your brain from 200 yards away if I asked him to.'

'Quite right, boss. It would be my absolute pleasure.'

'Goodbye, Mary Eno Pinchot Meyer,' said Gabrielli, standing. 'Please remember what I said. You let me down and you won't know what hits you, literally. It won't happen straight away, of course; we like to keep people on tenterhooks. I'm told that worry helps you lose weight, not that you need to, of course, with your figure. Remember, it could be anytime and anywhere. Your choice.' They all got up and left. Once they were outside, Giuseppe crept round to the back of her house where he had tapped into her phone line. He listened for a minute or two, but nothing. She wasn't phoning anybody. 'Drop us back at the hotel,' Gabrielli said to Mario, 'then you and Giuseppe come back and keep watch on her. Franco and Marco will relieve you at midnight.'

Chapter Eighteen
May 1961
The Vatican, Rome, Italy

'How is your campaign progressing?' the Pope asked Gabrielli during their now weekly phone calls, giving him progress reports.

'Excellent, I think, Holy Father. We have located and spoken to one of the women in your report, a Mary Meyer, and she made it clear that she is still having an affair with Kennedy. We have implemented stage one which I believe was successful. If not, however, we'll have to move on to stage two.'

'Do not, at any stage, implement stage three without my personal confirmation.'

'No, Holy Father, you have made that very clear.'

'So, what next?'

'We are making arrangements to visit a Miss Pamela Turnure, who works in the White House as a secretary. She works directly for Mrs. Kennedy.'

'You mean she works for Mrs. Kennedy during the day, and then arranges to meet and sleep with her husband outside of work hours?'

'Yes, Holy Father, that's exactly what I mean.'

'This wretched man has to be stopped, Gabrielli. He appears to have no decent morals or commitment to his marriage whatsoever. He is a complete disgrace to the sanctity of marriage, the church and to the Holy Catholic faith. If we're not careful, he will destroy us all.'

'I will talk personally with Miss Turnure as soon as possible.'

'Thank you, my son. Be assured, you are undoubtedly doing the Lord's work.'

Chapter Nineteen
May 25th, 1961
United States Congress, Washington D.C.

'I am announcing, in this address to the joint session of the United States Congress, full presidential support for the goal to "commit before this decade is out, to landing a man on the Moon, and returning him safely to the Earth" and I urge Congress to appropriate the necessary funds.'

For that, the President received a standing ovation. He finished his speech and his chauffeur drove him back to the White House, with Bobby joining him in the back of the long limousine. A black security car led the way with two more similar vehicles trailing along behind them. Jack leant forward in the limo and ensured the glass soundproof panel between the two of them, and the chauffeur and security detail sitting in the front, was shut completely tight. This ensured that anything said in the back of the car could not be overheard in the front.

'I'm telling you this in confidence, Bobby. My original idea was to propose to Congress today that NASA should attempt a manned mission to Mars, but NASA's Associate Administrator, a guy named Robert Seamans, spent the last three days and nights convincing me otherwise. The moon's not as glamorous or eye catching as Mars would be for the press, but I suppose we'll just have to settle for going to the moon for the time being.'

'You know, Jack, the Soviets say it can't be done. Not a return manned flight anyway. They reckon the spacecraft, or capsule I think it's called, will completely burn up during what's known as re-entry.'

'Hell, Bobby, what do they know?'

'Well, when it comes to space, Jack, at the moment, a hell of a lot more than we do.'

'Hell, it's NASA's problem now, not mine or yours, and as I said to you before, if it can't be done, we can always fake it. Build some place out in the desert behind a big fence, take a few photographs and then when we've got our "proof", bury everything. That'll really screw the Soviets. By the way, Bobby, changing the subject; I've arranged my first committee meeting now. Everything is in place. This Thursday evening. Can you make the necessary arrangements, please?'

'God, Jack, I feel like a damn pimp.'

'Sorry, Bobby, but someone's got to do it, and I can't. Jackie's got a meeting that'll keep her out all evening, and it's the only opportunity this week.'

'If I have to. Leave it with me, Jack.'

'You're a star, little bro!'

Chapter Twenty
June 1961
The Home of Pamela Turnure,
Washington D.C.

Pamela Turnure, as the First Lady's Press Secretary, was a highly trusted member of Jacqueline Kennedy's personal staff, but even then, she was not immune from the roving eye of the President. She was a Georgetown girl who many said resembled Jackie in lots of ways. According to the Pope's report which Gabrielli was now reading for the third time, Pamela Turnure had begun her affair with Kennedy when she was only 21.

Originally, she was the President's secretary when he was a senator, and Turnure only got the White House job thanks to Jack, who lobbied Jackie to hire her. Also, according to the report, unnamed sources in the White House said that whenever Jackie was away from the White House overnight, Pamela Turnure took her place in the President's bed. It was late afternoon in D.C. and the five men were now ready to tackle Pamela Turnure.

'Let's try a different approach here, Mario,' suggested Gabrielli. 'How about a series of telephone calls warning her off? She is not only close to the President and the First Lady, but she knows an awful lot of the security detail, and none of us can afford to be recognized. Giuseppe, can you get me through to her home telephone number and I'll have a quiet word in her ear.' They were sitting in two cars just around the corner and two streets away from Pamela Turnure's home, a single-story bungalow built of red brick, with a small garden at the front, and a much larger private one in the back. They still had the Lincoln, but they found they often needed two vehicles, so Gabrielli had rented a large Pontiac. Gabrielli left Marco and Franco to keep an eye on the cars while the other three hopped over a fence and made their way down a long alley that separated the backs of various gardens. Checking that it was all was clear and locating Pamela in the house through a pair of binoculars, Mario gave the thumbs-up sign and the three of them entered her garden through a back gate, where they headed for a large wooden shed located about 50 feet from the back of the house. Giuseppe Mancuso, their technical expert, then started to uncoil a long black cable, took one end and ran through the bushes to the side of the house where there was fortunately no window. He then connected his cable to the public telephone line junction where it went into Pamela Turnure's house. Returning quickly to the shed, he then connected the other end to a separate handheld telephone and dial now being held by Gabrielli.

'Just dial the number, boss, and you'll be straight through. Then signal me when you're done and I'll disconnect you.' And with that, he left the shed and, running through the bushes again, went back and crouched down next to the connection on the wall. Gabrielli did as had been suggested and a perky woman's voice on the other end answered after two rings.

'Pamela Turnure,' she chirped quite cheerfully.

'Good evening, Miss Turnure,' began Gabrielli, speaking in a very calm and gentle voice. 'My name is not important, but the message I have for you is. So please listen to it very carefully because I have no wish to repeat myself. Do you understand me so far, Miss Turnure?'

'Yes, I-I think so,' she stuttered back.

'Good. You will, from this moment on, cease your physical relationship with the President. If he asks to see you in private, make an excuse. Have a headache, feel ill, tell him you are worried that you have an illness he might catch. You can tell him anything you like but understand this, your relationship with him ends here, and it ends now. Have I made myself sufficiently clear or do I need to explain what will happen to you if you do not heed my warning?'

'No, no, I understand.'

'Let me assure you, Miss Turnure, if you wish to live to a ripe old age, then do not mention this telephone call to anyone, do not discuss it with anybody inside or outside of the White House, and if you should happen to mention it to any of the security detail, not only will you not live to a ripe old age, you will not see the end of the year. Understood?'

'Y-yes, completely,' she said, almost crying and shaking with fear.

'Excellent. Goodbye, Miss Turnure.'

Giuseppe was watching the shed from the side of the house where he was crouching, and at a signal from Gabrielli, he immediately disconnected the phone, pulled in and rolled up the cable. Then they all crept along behind the row of bushes at the back of the garden, out of the rear gate and returned to their car parked two streets away.

'I think she got the message, boss,' said Mario, smiling.

'OK, boys,' smiled Gabrielli. 'A job well done, I think. Now we try the same with Miss Sally Gilchrist.'

'Who's she?' asked Giuseppe.

'Oh, you'll like her,' said Gabrielli. 'She's what's known as an exotic dancer, or as we'd call her, a stripper in a nightclub. Apparently, the President pays frequent visits to the club, especially when Jackie's not around. And according to this report, she doesn't only dance for the President.'

They drove across town, met up with Marco and Franco again in their car, and all five of them entered the club in order to watch the delectable Miss Gilchrist (in the flesh, so to speak). Gabrielli could easily understand the President's interest. Sally Gilchrist was a 28-year-old stunner who would turn any man's head. There were color photographs of all the girls posted in glass frames outside the club, and the five men gave the pictures their undivided attention. Sally was about five feet nine inches tall, with long blonde hair, slim, and with the most fabulous assets, as Marco described her. They bought their tickets and entered the club where they were shown to a semi-circular padded booth, and ordered drinks while they watched the show. Half an hour into the show, Sally made her first appearance. She danced for a few minutes and then bit-by-bit, she slowly removed what little clothing she had been wearing. She left the stage after her performance, and disappeared backstage. Gabrielli also disappeared and followed her to her dressing room door. Mario and Franco were close behind him, while Giuseppe and Marco stood guard in the corridor to prevent anyone disturbing them. Gabrielli didn't knock; he just opened the dressing room door and walked in, with Mario and Franco behind him. Franco gently closed the dressing room door and turned the key that was in the lock. Sally was on her own and on hearing the door opening, she turned round and looked over her shoulder at the three men now in her dressing room. She didn't appear to be scared in any way and that, in itself, concerned Gabrielli. He was used to women being afraid of him and the boys, but Sally just turned her back on all three of them, watching them in her dressing table mirror as she spoke.

'I assume you three gentlemen want something?' she asked. 'Whatever it is, the answer is no, so clear off. I'm due back on stage in 20 minutes.'

'Well, you see, Miss Gilchrist, we don't like your answer, and I haven't even asked you a question yet, or more to the point; given you your instructions.'

'If you're trying to frighten me, I have to tell you, you're not succeeding. Look, whatever it is you want, spit it out, then clear off and leave me in peace.'

'We'll leave you in pieces if you don't pay attention, lady,' said Mario.

'Oh, very good,' said Gabrielli, 'a nice play on words.'

'Get on with it, will you; I don't have time to play guessing games.'

'Very well, Miss Gilchrist. You will cease all contact with President Kennedy with immediate effect, and never see him again. Clear enough?'

'Of course, honey,' she replied. 'Anything you say. Now please, and I am asking nicely, clear off and leave me alone.'

As she spoke, she leaned forward and pressed a button on the wall just above the surface of her dressing table. A very loud bell started ringing outside the room and, within 5 seconds, two of the club's muscular bouncers smashed the door down and burst into the room with two more behind them. Another two arrived at the end of the corridor and stood staring at Giuseppe and Marco, who were just standing there meekly as if this was nothing to do with them.

Inside the dressing room, Sally turned round and quietly said, 'Would you be kind enough to escort all these gentlemen out of the building, please? They have most definitely outstayed their welcome. Also, it might be an idea to have their pictures posted by the door so that they aren't accidentally let in again.'

'Are you sure you're alright, Sally?' asked one of the bouncers.

'Sure, I'm fine, Gus, just get rid of these creeps, will you, please?'

'I should point out, Miss Gilchrist, that ignoring my advice could be very costly,' said Gabrielli as he was being manhandled out of the dressing room.

'Yeah,' Sally replied dismissively. 'Well, when I want financial advice I'll talk to my bank manager. But thank you for your advice, which I am definitely choosing to ignore.'

At that point, the five men were unceremoniously escorted off the premises, with the club photographer grabbing a black and white pic of them as they left the building. 'So, what do we do now?' asked Mario, once they were back in the car.

'Now, I make a phone call,' answered Gabrielli.

Chapter Twenty-One
June 1961
The Vatican, Rome, Italy

Gabrielli had telephoned the Pope and told him about the problem of Sally Gilchrist. Pope John ordered him to leave the other four in Washington, but he, Gabrielli, should fly back to Rome and come to the Vatican as soon as practically possible. This matter was not something to talk about on the phone; it needed to be discussed face-to-face. He was now back in the Vatican, and sitting facing the Pope across his desk.

'What a great pity about Miss Gilchrist,' said the Pope. 'Are you one hundred percent sure there is no chance she will cooperate with us in time? Are you absolutely positive of the need to implement stage two?'

'To be perfectly frank, Holy Father,' replied Gabrielli, 'I think we could talk to that young woman until we all died of old age, and she still wouldn't listen to a word we say. She is the star of their show, and as such, she is constantly surrounded by a team of ten bouncers at the nightclub she works at. Not only that, she lives in a flat with two of the bouncers and one of the other strippers. Apart from when she is meeting with JFK, she is never alone without the bouncers. She feels secure and beyond our reach, but she doesn't realize just how far we are prepared to go.'

'So, you feel stage two is the only viable option we have in her case?'

'Yes, I'm afraid so, Holy Father.'

'Well, I do not wish to know any of the details, but please get it done as soon as possible, and perhaps it will be a lesson to the other women Kennedy meets with.'

'I will return to Washington on the next available flight and start making plans, but you do understand, Holy Father; stage two will take very careful planning and it cannot be rushed.'

'Yes, I do understand, Signor Gabrielli, but can you guarantee to me that stage two will definitely work?'

'Oh yes, without doubt. Stages two and three have never failed.'

'Yes, well let's just concentrate on stage two for the moment, shall we?'

'Of course. One other question before I leave, er, should I keep the Camerlengo informed of what I am doing, Holy Father?' asked Gabrielli.

'No, leave that to me, and in the meantime, have a good flight,' said the Pope, picking up his Bible to prepare for Mass later that day.

Chapter Twenty-Two

September 1961
The White House, Washington D.C.

The previous two and a half months had gone by quickly. Jack had addressed the North Atlantic Council, met with French President Charles de Gaulle in Paris, Adolf Scharf, the President of Austria, and had an interesting summit meeting with Soviet Premier Nikita Khrushchev. Jack had visited both the Queen and the British Prime Minister Harold Macmillan in London, and after returning to the States, he was now taking some time off and having a break. The major event of August, as far as Jack was concerned, happened not in the USA, but in Europe when the German Democratic Republic, or East Germany as Jack preferred to call it, started constructing what was being called the Berlin Wall on the 13th of August. The wall cut off by land, West Berlin from virtually all of surrounding East Germany and East Berlin. The barrier included guard towers placed along large concrete walls, accompanied by a wide-open area known as the "death strip" that contained anti-vehicle trenches, "fakir beds" and various other defenses. The Soviet-run Eastern Bloc was publicly portraying the wall as being erected to protect its population from severe fascist elements in the West that were conspiring to prevent the will of the people in building a strong socialist state in East Germany. The GDR authorities were officially referring to the wall as the Anti-Fascist Protection Rampart, and by implication, equating all the NATO countries and West Germany, in particular, with fascists. The West Berlin city government was having none of it, and they started openly calling it the Soviets "Wall of Shame". Jack liked the Berliners. Jack's "committee meetings" were working out very nicely, he thought, and the team Bobby had put together was working well. Jack varied the women he met in his various "meetings", and as he'd explained to Bobby, it was all about the need for a change.

'If I didn't need the variety, I'd be one hundred percent faithful to Jackie,' he'd told him. It wasn't all rest and relaxation as Jack was now busy preparing for his first address before the United Nations General Assembly. He was, as usual, playing around with words. He wasn't a wordsmith, but he was a great orator. He was brilliant at getting any audience on his side, but he usually needed his speechwriters to correct and put his own words into something a little more diplomatic. What he really wanted to say to the Soviet Union at the UN General Assembly was, "anything you can do, we can do better, so up yours" but both Bobby and the speechwriters felt that wasn't the most tactful thing to say. They had come back to him suggesting he talk about "challenging the Soviet Union, not to an arms race, but to a peace race". Jack liked that, and he felt sure he would get a rapturous round of applause from all the delegates except, perhaps, from the Soviets.

Chapter Twenty-Three
October 1961
The Willard Hotel, Washington D.C.

It had been nearly three and a half months since Claudio Gabrielli had his last meeting with the Pope, where he had received the Holy Father's official permission to prepare stage two, and when ready, put it into action. At long last, he was ready. The Pope didn't ask or want to know any details. He just wanted guaranteed assurance that nothing could ever be traced back to the Vatican. Utmost caution, he'd said, was far more important than speed. Hence, the three and a half months' preparation time.

Gabrielli and his team were still spending their nights in the Willard Hotel but during the day, they had been watching Sally Gilchrist go about her life as if the incident in her dressing room had never occurred. She was still sharing an apartment with one of the other dancers and two of the bouncers, but she'd not been able to see the President as he'd either been away on political trips to the UK, or on holiday with his wife and his family. Gabrielli's stage two option was very simple. Stage one was vocal persuasion, with added pressure applied if necessary. Stage two only came into play if stage one was a complete non-starter and in Sally Gilchrist's case, she'd not only made it clear stage one wasn't going to work, but she'd humiliated Gabrielli and his team in the process. So, stage two it was. Franco Lamberti's suggestion for implementing stage two was simple and quick; put a bullet through her brain. But this option had numerous risks. It was not only messy, but it carried with it the possible chance of being caught either in the act or trying to get away afterwards.

Even more serious, as far as Gabrielli was concerned, if caught, any one of them might mention, under torture (if, of course, it ever went that far) that their orders had originated from the Vatican. There was no proof, nothing in writing, of course, and obviously, even the slightest suggestion would be denied by anyone and everyone within the world of Catholicism, but nevertheless, it couldn't be risked. What Gabrielli needed was for Sally Gilchrist to simply disappear off the face of the earth, preferably without anybody knowing where she'd gone, whether it was of her own choice or not, or if she was ever intending to come back. If that was to happen, it meant, without doubt, starting by kidnapping her. So, Gabrielli set about planning a kidnap mission.

Kidnap is not easy, especially when your target lives and works with other people. So, the first thing to do was find out if she was ever alone. He put his team on the job doing alternate six-hour shifts. Marco and Franco together, and then they would be relieved by Mario and Giuseppe. When not watching, they would sleep so that they were fresh when they went back on watch. They had notebooks, and kept very strict records of any time Sally Gilchrist was seen totally alone. It never happened once during the first week, but it did happen just once during their second week of watching. On Friday evening, Sally left the club after her performance and stopped off at a grocery store on her way back to the apartment and spent fifteen minutes on food shopping. That was it. The only time during the entire two weeks she had not been with either her flat mate or the bouncers. The following week, again nothing. But then in week four, she stopped off at the grocery store again on the Friday night. This looked promising, so they continued to watch, getting more and more bored. But sure enough, the following week, she'd gone straight home on the Friday evening, but the next week, she yet again stopped off at the grocery store and spent somewhere between fifteen to thirty minutes doing her food shopping. Gabrielli then decided that while the boys were watching Sally, he would investigate the grocery store. So, the following morning, he walked inside the store, picked up a wire shopping basket and slowly walked round the inside of all the store's external walls, picking up a few food items here and there so as not to look suspicious. But he was mainly looking for any sort of room off to the side. Men's and women's toilets, storerooms, freezer rooms, an empty office; it didn't matter what sort of room as long as it was somewhere where they could grab her and get her away. Having done a complete circuit of the store, he paid for his few groceries and left, not wanting to draw attention to himself. Two days later, he wandered round again, this time stopping off in the men's toilet. The men's toilet was located next to a storeroom, which he could see, through its open door, had a loading bay at the back. It looked promising. The single cubicle in the toilet was positioned to the right of the single urinal, but in between them was a small window positioned about three feet above the floor. He estimated that the window was about eighteen inches wide and roughly two feet high, and opened out into the store's rear car park next to the loading bay. He paced from one side of the toilet to the other, measuring the length of the room, and then he did the same to get the approximate width. He made a few notes on a pad he carried in his pocket, and when the toilet was totally empty, he pulled a camera from his pocket and took a photograph of the toilet, ensuring to include the window. He then poked his head out of the window, looked both left and right, and then returned to the store. After paying for a loaf of bread, he left. The following day, Gabrielli took his undeveloped film, on which he'd taken several other photographs of any old houses he saw, and took it to the nearest film developers he could find. He casually chatted with the man behind the counter, telling him that he and his wife were buying an old house and doing it up. He got them to print all the pictures on the film, but he asked the developer if he could please give him a large blow-up version of the toilet picture, as he and his wife couldn't decide whether to demolish everything in the bathroom and start again, or play around with what was there. The developer did as he'd been requested and appeared to think nothing of it. Three days later, Gabrielli collected his photographs.

Over the next couple of weeks, when they weren't watching Sally, they were holed up in the hotel room working out precisely what to do. They knew they would take Sally on a Friday evening as that was when she always did her shopping. The plan was simple in that once they'd seen Sally enter the store, Marco would turn on his lothario skills and keep the female shop assistant busy until the deed was done. Mario and Franco would enter and hang around just inside the men's toilet, waiting to grab Sally as she walked past. To prevent her making a lot of noise, they'd chloroform her as they grabbed her. Once unconscious, they'd drag her into the toilet, while Giuseppe would ensure nobody else entered the toilet by sticking a prepared "Out of Order" sign on the door, and then standing guard. Once they'd pushed Sally out through the window, Gabrielli would help load her into the boot of the car. Mario would join Gabrielli in the front and take over the driving while Franco sat in the back. They would then drive around to the car park in front of the store where Marco and Giuseppe, having left the store, would then jump in the back with Franco. If all went well, they would be on their way within four minutes of Sally walking into the store. All of that was, to a certain extent, the easy bit, but what next?

'If we're getting rid of her permanently, boss,' said Franco, 'then she obviously has to be killed. I know Marco and Giuseppe don't like that side of this business so I can deal with that. But where do we dump her?'

'You mean what should we do with her poor dead body?' asked Giuseppe.

'That's what I just asked, didn't I?' replied an annoyed Franco.

'Calm, gentlemen,' said Gabrielli. 'Let's not fall out amongst ourselves. I think we have to either burn the corpse or bury it. My personal preference is to bury it. Burning produces smoke, and smoke can be seen for miles. Some nosey so-and-so might choose to investigate, and we can't risk that.'

'OK,' said Mario. 'So where?'

'It has to be somewhere really remote where she'll never be found in a million years,' responded Franco.

'You mean, like a desert, for example?' asked Gabrielli.

'The only desert I know of is the Mohave, and that's the other side of America near Las Vegas,' said Mario. 'I think it is too risky taking the body that far.'

'Agreed,' said Gabrielli.

'What about the Chihuahuan Desert?' asked Giuseppe. 'It's absolutely massive, and it covers parts of Mexico as well as the United States.'

'I've never heard of it,' said Gabrielli. 'Where exactly is it?'

'Well, I used to work for the telephone company in Texas, and I know the Chihuahuan occupies a lot of West Texas, plus parts of the Rio Grande Valley. I think there's a bit of it in Arizona as well, but I know both the Texas and Mexico areas are totally deserted. It's just too damned hot for anyone to ever go there.'

'Sounds ideal,' said Gabrielli. 'That's really good thinking, Giuseppe. We want to cross as few state borders as possible so from D.C., we can drop down into Virginia, drop south into Tennessee, west into Arkansas, and then cross into Texas. Once in Texas, we'll just drive into the desert somewhere, and bury her nice and deep.'

Chapter Twenty-Four
November 1961
The White House, Washington D.C.

Jack was busy working at his desk in the Oval office when the door suddenly opened unannounced and Bobby walked in.

'Hi, Jack,' he muttered.

'Are you telling me somebody's taken over an airplane, or are you just simply saying hello? Just saying Hijack can be a bit confusing,' his brother replied.

'Oh, yeah, never occurred to me. I'm just saying hello, so no need to panic.'

'Thank God for that.'

'Talking of God reminds me. Have you heard any more from that Bishop O'Boyle or has the Pope given up trying to change your sordid habits?'

'Sorry, Bobby, I meant to tell you but life has been a bit hectic since we got back from holiday. Mary told me on the phone that she got a visit from some guy threatening her and telling her that if she didn't stay away from me, she'd suffer the consequences.'

'Is she OK?' asked Bobby.

'Yeah, but she's scared witless. She's no idea who these people are, but she said he spoke with what she thought was an Italian accent.'

'That means the Vatican, Jack.'

'Really Bobby,' replied his brother. 'I'm not sure. I can't believe the church would resort to strong-arm tactics. Anyway, then Pamela got a phone call telling her to stay out of my bed, or else. Damn cheek. It scared her for a while, and to be honest, with me being away, there hasn't been a chance to get together anyway. It may be the Vatican, but I'd like to think the church is above threats and violence.'

'Let's face it, Jack, the Catholic Church has done an awful lot of violent things over the centuries if it feels threatened and according to Bishop O'Boyle, the Pope sees your philandering as a threat to the Catholic church's reputation. Under those circumstances, I wouldn't put anything past them. Be careful, Jack, be very careful.'

Chapter Twenty-Five
November 1961
The Willard Hotel, Washington D.C.

The five men sat in the lobby of their hotel, looking at the big clock on the wall. They'd just finished a cup of tea; a habit they'd gotten into in Rome. It was nearly 6.30 on a Friday evening and they were just about ready to leave. The grocery store they were heading for was one of the 7-Eleven chains that were sprouting up all over the United States. They all varied in size, but the one thing they all had in common was the fact that they kept exceedingly long opening hours; some were even open 24 hours a day, seven days a week. The clock in the lobby struck the half hour, and they all got up and headed for the car. Mario and Franco had been out earlier in the afternoon and had stolen a large station-wagon-style car from a parking lot. They'd changed the number plates within an hour of the theft. The large dark maroon Buick looked anonymous enough, and Gabrielli felt that, providing they kept well within the speed limits, they were highly unlikely to get stopped by anyone.

The particular 7-Eleven Gabrielli and his team were now heading for was the one where Sally Gilchrist stopped off every other Friday evening and did her grocery shopping. They were frantically hoping tonight was not going to be an exception to the rule, as a lot of planning and preparation had gone into getting everything ready. They pulled into the front car park, and the four men all got out, leaving Gabrielli to drive the car round to the rear car park. Mario and Franco went straight into the shop, with Marco and Giuseppe following on behind them. Marco stopped at the till and started flirting with the girl behind it while Giuseppe went and stood looking at the food on the shelves close to the gents' toilet entrance. Mario and Franco had already disappeared into the toilet. Sally arrived at her usual time and casually strolled into the shop, picking up one of their wire baskets en-route. She slowly walked down the left aisle, and just as she got to the entrance to the gents', Giuseppe nodded his head and Mario and Franco, who had been watching for his signal through the slightly ajar door, suddenly burst through the gents' toilet door and into the shop. Franco grabbed Sally round the head with his left hand, while holding a cloth soaked in chloroform to her nose and mouth with his right hand. Mario had grabbed her with both arms round her waist, and the two of them dragged her backwards, kicking and screaming into the toilet.

Her resistance didn't last long as the chloroform quickly took effect, and within ten seconds, she was out cold. Outside the toilet, Giuseppe had stuck his "Out of Order" notice on the toilet door with a drawing pin, and he then walked back to the front of the shop where he casually collected Marco. Once the two of them were out of sight from the shop, they ran round to the rear of the building. Back inside the toilet, Mario had pushed open the window, and then he and Franco lifted Sally's unconscious body out through the narrow gap into the waiting arms of Gabrielli and Giuseppe who had now joined him. The two of them then carried the unconscious woman over to the car, pushed her into the open boot or trunk area in the rear of the station wagon, covered her over with a couple of blankets, and finally, they closed the back door of the car. They all then piled in the back of the Buick with Mario at the wheel, and sped away from the 7-Eleven, heading for Texas.

About ten miles outside of Washington, they pulled over into a quiet side street, and Franco gave Sally another dose of chloroform. They kept this procedure up for several hours, alternating drivers in two or three-hour shifts, knowing that the journey in total would probably take them 24 hours. Once they'd safely crossed the border into Texas, they started the long drive to the edge of the Chihuahuan Desert. At roughly

8.00 pm on the Saturday night, with the sun sinking fast, they found a suitable spot.

'OK, everyone, this'll do nicely,' said Gabrielli. 'Let's start digging.' They got out of the car and the four assistants dug a hole roughly six-foot long, two-foot wide and at least seven-foot deep.

'That's deep enough,' commanded Gabrielli 'Let's put her body in the ground, and Franco will make sure she never bothers us again.'

Mario and Franco took Sally's limp body out of the car and literally threw her into the hole. Franco, pulling what looked like a large bowie knife out of a sheath, jumped in on top of her and proceeded to slit her throat from ear-to-ear.

'Don't worry, Giuseppe,' said Gabrielli. 'I know you hate all this, but I assure you, it was necessary, and she wouldn't have known a thing about it.' They covered her body with soil, filled in the hole, moved a few rocks over the disturbed area, and then brushed the surface dirt with a few branches. Getting back into the car, they started the long, boring return journey to Washington D.C., where they eventually dumped the Buick station wagon in a side street and walked back to the Willard Hotel.

Chapter Twenty-Six
November 1961
The Vatican, Rome, Italy

Pope John XXIII was reading his Bible and praying in preparation for that evening's mass when the phone in his private office rang. This was the only telephone in the entire Vatican that did not go through a switchboard, and the Pope knew only one person in the world knew the number. 'Good evening, Signor Gabrielli,' he answered, picking up the receiver.

'Good evening, Holy Father,' he replied. 'It gives me no pleasure in reporting this, Holy Father, but in the matter of Miss Gilchrist, stage two has been completed.'

'It gives me no pleasure in hearing it, my son, but you have done what needed to be done. Can I assume there were no problems?'

'Indeed you can, Holy Father. As you know, it took a long time to plan, but once we put the plan into operation, it took place without a hitch, and nobody will ever know why Miss Gilchrist disappeared, and they will forever wonder where she has moved to.'

'You have done well, Signor. Please accept both mine and the church's thanks in this matter. There are times in life when one is forced to do things one would rather not do. But on some occasions, what must be done, must be done. This was one of those occasions. What next?'

'There is some talk that a certain actress has attracted the President's eye, and I am going to look into the matter. I will, of course, keep you informed, Holy Father.'

'Thank you, my son, and may God continue to bless you in your work.'

Chapter Twenty-Seven
January 1962
The White House, Washington D.C.

'I sincerely hope, Bobby,' began Jack, the minute his brother walked through the door of the Oval Office, 'that 1962 doesn't have as many pitfalls as 1961 threw at us. We really could have done without the Bay of Pigs fiasco. It made America look stupid and it made me look totally incompetent. Then there was Gagarin becoming the first man in space. That made us look inferior to Khrushchev's almighty flaming Soviet Union.'

'OK, there were a couple of blips, Jack, but overall you had a good year. Your most recent overseas trips were all successful. Venezuela and Columbia were successful meetings, and you had a good meeting with the British Prime Minister again in Bermuda. Things could be a lot worse, Jack, and you've got a lot of things to look forward to this year.'

'I know, I guess I'm just a bit nervous about the State of the Union address next week. It's not the talking bit, I love that; it's just the content. Will it be enough?'

'Well, you can tell Congress that next month NASA is sending John Glenn into space on Friendship 7 to become the first American to orbit the earth.'

'True, but I thought it was called the Mercury Atlas?' asked Jack with a frown.

'That's the rocket it's powered by, Jack,' smiled Bobby. 'A Mercury Atlas 6. The capsule Glenn will be in is called Friendship 7.'

'How the hell do you remember all this stuff, Bobby?'

'I don't have as much pressure on me, Jack,' he replied. 'Look, getting back to your State of the Union address. You've had some great successes. Make sure you mention that you established the Peace Corps. That's been brilliant. As for the economy, make sure you mention the yearly inflation rate in the USA was only 1.07% whereas, in the UK for example, it was just short of 3%. A gallon of gas is only 27 cents in America, and the average cost of a brand-new car in the U.S. is only $2,850 U.S. dollars. Let's face it, Jack, the people of America are having it really good under your Presidency. You shouldn't hold back in saying so, and you make sure you tell that to the congressmen.'

'Whatever you say, Bobby. Should I mention Big Ivan? What do you think?'

'You can't ignore the fact, Jack, that back in October, the Soviet Union conducted the largest ever nuclear bomb test the world has ever seen, despite worldwide objections. I'm told the strength of that blast was equivalent to over 50 million tons of T.N.T, and it registered at 5.0 on the Richter scale.'

'This can't go on,' said Jack. 'It's getting ridiculous. I'm thinking of proposing a nuclear test ban treaty. I'm pretty sure the UK would agree, but there's no point if the Soviets won't sign up to it.'

'Great idea, bro,' said Bobby. 'But perhaps it's a bit too soon after Big Ivan was set off. The Soviets will just say you're running scared.'

'Hell Bobby, I am scared. But you're right; we can't let them know that.'

'Hold fire on that one for the moment, Jack, and wait till the timing is right. One thing you can and should definitely mention though in your State of the Union address is that segregation on all railways in the south has now ended. That really is something the whole country should celebrate.'

'I know,' began Jack, 'that when the UN General Assembly condemned apartheid, they were principally aiming their comments at South Africa, but I'm glad we're doing our bit for racial equality and civil rights in America, even if some don't like it.'

'I don't know who it was, but whoever said it was right when they said, "you can't please all of the people all of the time".'

'Wow Bobby,' smiled Jack. 'Something you don't know? I'm truly amazed!'

'Tell me, Mr. President, is it permissible under the terms of the Constitution of the United States of America for younger brothers to beat up their older brothers in retaliation for suffering crimes of extreme verbal abuse?'

'No,' replied Jack, laughing. 'I'm sure that's not allowed under the Constitution.'

'I think I'm going to check,' said Bobby, laughing.

'You do that,' said Jack. 'You do that.'

Chapter Twenty-Eight
January 1962
FBI Headquarters, Washington D.C.

In his office, J. Edgar Hoover, the undisputed head of the FBI was reading through a file. What he was reading both shocked and delighted him at the same time. John Edgar Hoover had been appointed the first-ever Director of the Federal Bureau of Investigation back in 1924. He'd survived through numerous Presidents who came and went, but he was still there. He'd seen off Calvin Coolidge, Herbert Hoover, Franklin D. Roosevelt, Harry S. Truman, Dwight D. Eisenhower, and he was pretty sure he'd be around long after John Fitzgerald Kennedy had left the White House.

The new Attorney General, Bobby Kennedy, he knew was not a fan of his, and he also knew that the Attorney General suspected him of secretive abuses of his power. J. Edgar didn't care, and as far as he was concerned, the end always justified the means. Because of his personal philosophy, he used the FBI to harass political dissenters and activists, he amassed secret files on any and all political leaders, and if it was the only way, he would quite happily collect evidence using illegal methods. Because of all this, J. Edgar now considered himself to be untouchable, as he had amassed a great deal of power and was in a position to intimidate and threaten any sitting president, including the current one.

Back in 1956, Hoover was becoming increasingly frustrated by several decisions of the U.S. Supreme Court that had limited the Justice Department's ability to prosecute people for their political opinions, most notably communists. Some of Hoover's aides reported that he would deliberately exaggerate the threat of communism to "ensure financial and public support for the FBI". It was during this time that J. Edgar formalized a covert "dirty tricks" program under the name "Cointelpro" which was first used to disrupt the Communist Party of the USA. Hoover went after targets that ranged from suspected everyday spies to larger celebrity figures such as Charlie Chaplin, in fact; anyone that he saw as spreading Communist Party propaganda. "Cointelpro's" illegal methods included infiltration, burglaries, illegal wiretaps, planting forged documents, spreading false rumors about key members of target organizations, inciting violence and even on rare occasions, arranging murders.

It was now January 1962, and as he sat at his desk, J. Edgar was smiling to himself. He was reading a report informing him that the new President, who everyone seemed to love and admire, but who J. Edgar personally disliked intensely, was apparently having secret affairs with numerous different women. He wouldn't make this knowledge public of course, but like so many of the files and reports he had in his possession, he would file it away and only bring it out if needed. That way, he was the one in control, not JFK.

Chapter Twenty-Nine
February 1962
The Willard Hotel, Washington D.C.

Gabrielli was sick and tired of Washington D.C. He was missing Italy, and in particular, he missed Rome. He missed the romance of Italy, the music, the art, the food, the people, and yes, he missed the church and the Vatican. Despite how he earned his living, he still considered himself to be a religious man, and he followed Catholic doctrine to the best of his ability. Confession was, of course, extremely important for him, but in view of the nature of his current activities, he felt he couldn't share any of this in a confessional with a priest he didn't know, just in case, so he kept his more serious confessions to his rare visits to update the Holy Father personally. He had news for Pope John XXIII, in that they had a brand-new target in their sights. That target was a young woman he knew for a fact JFK was consorting with named Judith Campbell.

The team of investigators the Pope had employed to prepare the original report into John Fitzgerald Kennedy didn't stop working for him when they submitted their initial report. At the Pope's request, they had continued to investigate and then record their findings in the form of monthly written reports. However, they no longer submitted their reports to the Holy Father and instead, they put the reports inside a stiff, unmarked brown envelope, which they then left inside a secure locker in bag storage at Washington's Union Station located at 50 Massachusetts Avenue. They dropped off their report on the last day of every month, and Gabrielli himself collected the reports on the first day of every following month. The lead investigator and Gabrielli were the only two people with keys to the locker. According to the new information he now had in this month's report, Frank Sinatra had introduced JFK to Judith Campbell, a Californian girl and an ex of Sinatra's. The president met her in 1960 at the Sands Hotel in Las Vegas, where Sinatra was performing at the time. Again, according to Gabrielli's information, JFK paid attention only to her. One thing that did concern him in the report however, and that sources had suggested, that Campbell had apparently ferried envelopes from JFK to the mob. The report stated that the envelopes were "alleged" payoffs or instructions for vote-buying in elections, and plans to kill Fidel Castro. Gabrielli had no way of knowing if any of this was true, but one thing he did know was that he didn't want to cross the mob. Continuing to read the report he had in front of him, it said that Judith Campbell was a Los Angeles socialite, who had previously dated Frank Sinatra, began her affair with Kennedy during his 1960 Presidential campaign, and that they were still continuing their relationship, even though JFK was now resident in the White House. To Gabrielli's mind, it was now time to issue yet another warning to yet another woman involved with John F. Kennedy.

Where the hell did the man get his stamina from, he wondered to himself.

'Get everyone together, Mario,' commanded Gabrielli. 'We're all off on our travels again. It's time for another warning to be issued. Why don't you ask Franco to bring that rather nice Bowie knife of his with him?'

'I'm sure it will be a pleasure for him, boss.' The five of them left the hotel and walked round to their car which was now kept in an underground car park next to the hotel. Nobody could see it down there.

'Where exactly are we going, boss?' enquired Giuseppe.

'The airport, and then Los Angeles,' replied Gabrielli.

On the aircraft, Gabrielli, who had paid for two seats so that he could have the window seat to himself, and keep the one next to it empty, started to read the highly sensitive report on Judith Campbell that he'd picked up from the Union

Station locker. He read through all the preamble about where she'd been born, grew up, school days etc., and he'd read a bit about her many meetings with JFK. But he was now getting to what he considered to be the most exciting and interesting part; her meetings with members of the mob. There was a note in the report at this point stating that everything mentioned from this point on should only be treated as possible background information as it was all just hearsay. He-said-she-said-type conversations with people who overheard someone else say etc. "Hardly reliable, but it may prove useful" the report said. The report read as follows:

Judith Campbell's first assignment as a mob courier was suggested by JFK at dinner in his Georgetown house on April 6, 1960. Jackie, then pregnant with John Jr., was away in Florida. Campbell said she felt uncomfortable making love with Kennedy in the bed he shared with his wife. However, she had also apparently said, 'My interest in Jack, and my need to be with him, was stronger than my conscience.' A third person, a lobbyist named Bill, was at dinner that night.

'He and Jack spent the entire evening discussing strategy for the West Virginia primary,' said Campbell. 'That was the one he was really worried about because he was Catholic and running against Hubert Humphrey, a Protestant, in a state that was 95 percent Protestant. Jack and the lobbyist talked about getting money into West Virginia and about who had influence in the state. In the middle of their conversation, Jack turned to Campbell and said, 'Could you quietly arrange a meeting with Sam for me?'

'Why, or shouldn't I ask?' responded Campbell, not knowing that Sam was in fact Sam Giancana, Chicago's Godfather. Campbell said she assumed that Kennedy was well aware of Sam's identity.

JFK reportedly said, at this point, 'I think I may need his help in the campaign.' He wanted the meeting as soon as possible and gave me a few dates that were good for him.

Pleased to be of help, Campbell called Giancana the next morning and said she'd like to talk to him in Chicago. She arrived at 8:30 a.m. on April 8ᵗʰ and talked to Sam at a Chicago club, where she told Sam that Jack wanted to meet with him because he needed his help in the campaign. Sam agreed to the meeting, and the date was set for four days later at the Fontainebleau in Miami Beach. Campbell called Jack to tell him, then flew to Miami because Kennedy wanted her to be there.

Gabrielli wasn't at all sure how much of this dialogue and various overheard conversations he could believe, but nevertheless, it was fascinating. He kept reading.

Kennedy met with Giancana at the Fontainebleau on April 12. Campbell was not present at the meeting, but according to the report, Jack went to her suite afterward, and she asked him how the meeting had gone. He seemed very happy about it and thanked her for making the arrangements. He then stayed with her for an hour or so. As Kennedy was leaving, he handed Campbell an envelope, telling her not to open it until he was gone. Inside, she found two $1,000 bills. Apparently, it was to pay for the new mink coat Campbell had worn to his house in Georgetown.

After Kennedy received the nomination in July, he asked Campbell to arrange several more meetings with Giancana. At least one of them, at the Navarro Hotel in New York in early August, had to do with the general election. Reputedly, Campbell had claimed in a conversation, 'After Jack was elected, Sam kept saying Kennedy would never have been President if it hadn't been for his efforts on Kennedy's behalf in Cook County, Illinois.' An overwhelming turnout for Kennedy in Cook County enabled him to carry Illinois by a slim 8,858 votes.

In the early months of his Administration, Kennedy had little time for Campbell. During this period, the presence of a Communist regime in nearby Cuba was becoming a major political issue. A few days after the bungled Bay of Pigs invasion, Kennedy called Campbell in California and asked her to fly to Las Vegas to pick up an envelope from Johnny

Roselli, Giancana's right hand man, which she was to deliver to Giancana in Chicago. Once there, she arranged a meeting between the President and the Mafia boss. The report stated that the meeting took place in Campbell's suite at the Ambassador East on April 28.

The report then reiterated once again that none of these apparent conversations can be proved one way or the other, but the investigators are simply reporting what they've heard and been told, even though it may often be second or third hand.

On April 29, at Kennedy's request, Campbell flew to Florida, where she had drinks with Giancana and Roselli, who were there for a meeting. She picked up another envelope from them and returned to Washington on May 4th. Campbell then called the White House and asked for Evelyn Lincoln, who put her right through to the President. They made arrangements for delivering the envelope the following day. That next day, Campbell went to the White House for lunch. She was shown into the family quarters, where she and Dave Powers made small talk while Kennedy took a swim. After lunch, Kennedy escorted Campbell into the master bedroom. As he was showing her out, just over an hour later, Kennedy gave Campbell another envelope he wanted delivered to Giancana.

For days and sometimes weeks at a time that spring and summer, Campbell crisscrossed the country by train and plane at her own expense, carrying plain 9" by 12" manila envelopes from Kennedy to Giancana and Roselli and back again. The investigator's report stated that there was no writing on the envelopes, no labels, no stamped address, nothing. They weighed about the same as a weekly magazine and probably contained papers, but nobody knew for sure because nobody ever saw inside them. Blindly accepting her role as the President's personal messenger, Campbell never questioned what she was being asked to do.

As the summer progressed, Kennedy grew more preoccupied with the problems of the Presidency. He was criticized for not coming across as a strong and decisive leader at his first meeting with an intransigent Soviet Premier Khrushchev in Vienna. Then, in August, the East Germans erected the Berlin Wall. A distracted Kennedy grew more imperious with Campbell. He also grossly offended her during an August meeting at the White House. In front of presidential aide Dave Powers, Kennedy asked Campbell if she had told anyone about a night the year before when he had suggested a ménage à trois, and she had refused. She was annoyed at this becoming public, but she still agreed to pick up one more envelope from Giancana and Roselli and to bring it back to the White House. There, the report then claimed, in the big double bed in the family quarters on August 24, Kennedy presented Campbell with a diamond-and-ruby brooch as a thank you gift.

Bringing the report up to date, it stated that early in 1962, their relationship had begun to sour, and Campbell had told one of the investigators in confidence that she was very lonely a lot of the time, going with a married man. Also, she was raised a Catholic and knew that such an illicit relationship was wrong in the eyes of God, but she supposed she rationalized things because Jack had said his "marriage was unhappy and divorce was a possibility". Though she had visited Kennedy about twenty times at the White House, Campbell was now starting to resent the suggestion that she was supposed to jump every time the President called.

Gabrielli felt his timing was perfect. They had her home address, and as usual, they parked around the corner and out of sight of the house. Gabrielli took Franco with him, and the two of them went around the corner, along the street and up the driveway to her front door. Franco pushed the doorbell, and a few seconds later, Judith Campbell opened the door. She took one look at the two men standing in front of her, both dressed in dark suits, white shirts, navy ties and wearing sunglasses, and she assumed they were both FBI agents.

'Oh, for God's sake, will you guys tell J. Edgar bloody Hoover to leave me alone? I've answered every damn question and told you everything you wanted to know about the President, Sam Giancana and Johnny Roselli.'

'Nevertheless, may we please come in Miss Campbell?' asked Gabrielli, who was dying to know how much the FBI knew, so he decided to play along and pretend they were both FBI as well. 'As you have correctly surmised,' began Gabrielli looking at Franco to ensure he played along, 'my colleague and I are both with the FBI, and we would be grateful if you would just answer one or two additional questions for us.'

'Look, I know Sam Giancana and Johnny Roselli are under investigation by you people, but I promise you, I know nothing more than I have already told you.'

'OK,' said Gabrielli very gently. 'If I'm not being too delicate Miss Campbell, may I please ask the current state of your relationship with the President? As you can imagine, it is not something the FBI, or the White House would like made public. But with the ongoing investigations into Giancana and Roselli, there is always the possibility that something will leak out.'

'I assure you agent...'

'Oh, I'm so sorry, Miss Campbell, we didn't introduce ourselves. I am senior agent Morrelli, and this gentleman is agent Visconti. As you have probably gathered from our names, both our families migrated to the United States from Italy several generations ago. Now, your relationship with the President?'

Gabrielli was keen to keep the conversation moving before she asked to see their ID, which, of course, neither of them had.

'Oh, you can tell J. Edgar not to worry about me. I hardly ever see Jack anymore, and when I do, he's not as fit as he used to be. Being perfectly frank, agent Morrelli, I think we've more than run our course.'

'Excellent news, Miss Campbell,' Gabrielli said. 'Can I assure the Director that your liaisons with the President are now finished?'

'Well, I may have to see him once or twice more in the next couple of weeks, just to tidy up one or two matters, but I assure you that will not involve anything intimate anymore. No, I shall be heading back here to sunny California permanently for a much quieter life. Well, at least quieter than it has been here.' With that, Gabrielli and Franco left, with Judith Campbell knowing nothing about them and thinking she'd just had yet another visit from the FBI. Another job well done.

Chapter Thirty
March 1962
The White House, Washington D.C.

Evelyn knocked on the door of the Oval Office and walked in without waiting for a reply. Jack had recently told her to do so, having gotten fed up with constantly trying to shout loud enough to be heard on the other side of the thick door.

'Good morning, Mr. President,' she began. 'I just wanted to check with you about your visit to Palm Springs this month. I can't see any official appointments, and I just wanted to be sure I hadn't missed anything?'

'No, you're fine, Evelyn,' Jack replied. 'The Palm Springs' trip is just a few days break in peace and quiet where I can compose a few speeches without being interrupted every ten minutes.'

'Like I'm doing now,' said Bobby, walking through the door.

'Thank you, Evelyn,' said Jack, and she left, closing the door behind her.

'Tell me, Jack,' asked his brother. 'Why are you really going to Palm Springs? I know you, and if you want peace and quiet to put some thoughts together for a speech you do it upstairs in the privacy of the house.' \

'Do you remember that dinner party I went to last month in New York?'

'Yeah, of course I do. It was in your honor.'

'Well, during the evening, I met one of the guests; a certain young film actress named Marilyn Monroe. We hit it off really well. I got her to give me her number before she left and I've invited her to Palm Springs where sadly, Jackie is unable to join us.'

'So how the hell are you going to organize this one, Jack?'

'I've managed to borrow Bing Crosby's house, although he doesn't know, of course, that Marilyn will be staying for the weekend.'

'Does she know she's staying for the weekend and why?'

'Not a hundred percent sure, but I think she's got a pretty good idea.'

'God, Jack,' said his brother. 'Your flaming libido will be the death of you.'

Marilyn Monroe's birth name was Norma Jeane Mortenson, and she was born in Los Angeles on the 1st of June, 1926. She was, at that moment in time, the most famous American actress, model, and singer in the United States, and probably the world. She was most famous for playing ditsy comic "blonde bombshell" characters, and she had become one of the most popular sex symbols of the 1950s and now, the 1960s. She was, without doubt, an icon of the era's attitudes towards sexuality.

Born and raised in Los Angeles, Marilyn spent most of her childhood in various foster homes and an orphanage. She got married to James Dougherty at the age of just sixteen. While working in a radio-plane factory in 1944 as part of the war effort, she was introduced to a photographer from the First Motion Picture Unit and she began a very successful pin-up modelling career. The modelling work led to short-lived film contracts with Twentieth Century Fox in 1946 and 1947 and then Columbia Pictures in 1948. After a series of minor film roles, she signed a new contract with Fox in 1951. Over the next two years, she became a popular actress and had roles in several comedies, including "As Young as You Feel" and "Monkey Business", and in the dramas, "Clash by Night" and "Don't Bother to Knock". Marilyn faced a scandal when it was revealed that she had posed for nude photos before she became a star, but the story did not tarnish her career and instead resulted in massively increased interest in her films.

By 1953, Marilyn was one of the most marketable Hollywood stars, and she had leading roles in the film "Niagara", which focused on her enormous sex appeal, and two good comedies in "Gentlemen Prefer Blondes" and "How to Marry a Millionaire", which established her star image as a "dumb blonde". Although she played a significant role in the creation and management of her public image throughout her career, she was disappointed when she was typecast and grossly underpaid by the studio. She was briefly suspended in early 1954 for refusing a film project but returned to star in one of the biggest box office successes of her career, "The Seven-Year Itch".

When the studio was still reluctant to change Marilyn's contract, she founded her own film production company in late 1954 and named it Marilyn Monroe Productions, or MMP. She dedicated 1955 to building her company and began studying method acting at the Actors Studio. In late 1955, Fox eventually awarded her a new contract, which gave her more control and a much larger salary. Her subsequent roles included a critically acclaimed performance in "Bus Stop" and the first independent production of MMP, "The Prince and the Showgirl". In mid-1957, Marilyn fell pregnant. Sadly, the pregnancy was ectopic and had to be terminated. Marilyn also suffered a miscarriage a year later. Her gynecological problems were largely caused by something called endometriosis, a disease from which she suffered throughout her adult life. Marilyn was also briefly hospitalized during this time due to a barbiturate overdose. Marilyn won a Golden Globe for "Best Actress" for her work in "Some Like It Hot" in 1959, which was both a critical and commercial success for her. Her latest completed film was the drama "The Misfits" which was released in 1961. Sadly, Marilyn's troubled private life was now receiving far too much attention. She struggled with substance abuse, regular depression and massive anxiety attacks. Her second marriage to retired baseball star Joe DiMaggio in 1954 had ended in divorce a year later, and her third marriage to the playwright Arthur Miller in 1956 had also ended in divorce in 1961. Jack thought Marilyn was the sexiest woman he'd ever met, and he couldn't wait for his trip to Palm Springs. Unfortunately for Marilyn, Gabrielli had found out about the trip as well, and he'd decided action needed to be taken in the near future.

President John Fitzgerald Kennedy

Jacqueline Kennedy

Bobby Kennedy

Nikita Khrushchev

Pope John XXIII

Cardinal Benedetto
Massela

Pope John VI

Bishop Patrick O'Boyle

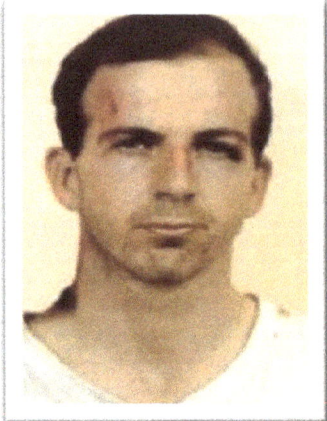

Lee Harvey Oswald   Jack Ruby

Five seconds before the impact of the first shot

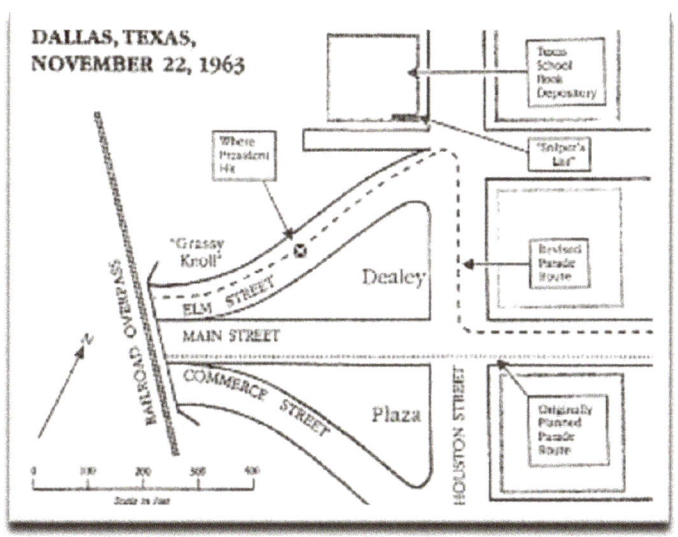

DALLAS, TEXAS,
NOVEMBER 22, 1963

Chapter Thirty-One
March 1962
The Vatican, Rome, Italy

Pope John XXIII was thinking about his job. Yes, he was the Pope and he was God's chosen vessel here on earth, and yes, he was following in the footsteps of all the Popes that had gone before him, and the Apostle Peter before all of them, but however you care to describe it, it was still a job.

There were myriads of things he could do every day. There were myriads of things he chose to do, but there was nothing he actually had to do. After all, he was the Pope, the boss, the big cheese, the man-in-charge, and his decision in all matters was final. One of the first things the Pope had done on being "chosen" was to read up on the subject of Papal infallibility within the Catholic Church. Papal infallibility is a total mystery to non-Catholics, but it is a dogma of the Catholic Church that states that, in virtue of the promise of Jesus to Peter, the Pope is preserved from the possibility of error "when, in the exercise of his office as shepherd and teacher of all Christians, in virtue of his supreme apostolic authority, he defines a doctrine concerning faith or morals to be held by the whole Church". This "sacred doctrine" was defined dogmatically at the First Ecumenical Council of the Vatican of 1869–1870, but it had been defended long before that, existing already in medieval theology and being the majority opinion at the time of the Counter-Reformation. In other words, he was never wrong in anything he said or did.

According to all the Catholic theology he'd read, there were several concepts important to the understanding of infallible, divine revelation: Sacred Scripture, Sacred

Tradition, and the Sacred Magisterium. The infallible teachings of the Pope are part of the Sacred Magisterium, which also consists of ecumenical councils and the "ordinary and universal magisterium". In Catholic theology, papal infallibility is one of the channels of the infallibility of the Church. The infallible teachings of the Pope must be based on, or at least not contradict, Sacred Tradition or Sacred Scripture.

The doctrine of infallibility relies on one of the cornerstones of Catholic dogma: that of the supremacy of the pope stretching all the way back to the Apostle Peter, and his authority as the ruling agent who decides what are accepted as formal beliefs in the Roman Catholic Church. The use of this power is referred to as speaking *ex cathedra*. The solemn declaration of papal infallibility by Vatican I took place on 18 July 1870. Since that time, the only example of an *ex cathedra* decree took place in 1950, when Pope Pius XII defined the Assumption of Mary as an article of faith. Prior to the solemn definition of 1870, there were other decrees which fit the definition of *ex cathedra*. For example, Pope Boniface VIII in the bull *Unam Sanctam* of 1302, and Pope Pius IX in the Papal constitution *Ineffabilis Deus* of 1854.

Having read and studied all of this at length, the Holy Father came to the conclusion that what he was doing, or more accurately, what his agents were doing in the United States on behalf of both himself and the worldwide Catholic Church, was indeed holy in that everything they were doing was without doubt, for the benefit of the entire Catholic community worldwide. Not that any of this would ever come out and be made public of course but if it did, he decided, he would simply claim the actions he'd decreed came under the terms of Papal infallibility, which clearly stated that he could define a doctrine concerning faith or "morals" to be held by the whole Church, and surely that's what was being carried out on the Church's behalf in America.

The Pope picked up the telephone on his desk and asked the voice on the other end to find the Camerlengo and have him come to his private quarters as soon as possible. Cardinal Masella arrived about ten minutes later and found the Holy Father sitting on a sofa in his sitting room.

'Ah, good morning, Benedetto. Please, take a seat,' the Pope said pointing at the armchair next to him.

'Good morning to you too, Angelo,' he replied, collapsing into the seat. 'I'm really starting to notice my age you know, and all those stairs really don't help. What can I do for you, my friend?' he asked.

'I thought I should bring you up-to-date with what has been happening in the United States. It is now fourteen months since I first called in Signor Claudio Gabrielli. During that time, he and his team from the Holy Office have been very successful, and they have achieved a tremendous amount, but they have, of necessity, had to take certain actions which I am sure you and I would find most distasteful and unpleasant.'

'But you did say of necessity?' queried the Camerlengo.

'I did, and I believe they have done everything they can to control this rogue Catholic President's immoral behavior, for that, I believe, is what he is; a totally immoral rogue Catholic. Despite over a year of extremely hard work, the President's attitude to women does not appear to have changed one iota.'

'So, if I may ask, what has Signor Gabrielli been doing exactly?'

'He has been doing everything he can to prevent the President's indiscretions happening and becoming public knowledge,' answered the Pope. 'Most of this has been achieved by having quiet conversations with all the various women involved, and you would not believe, my friend, just how many women there are. I understand from Signor Gabrielli that in most cases, these have been calm and reasoned conversations, but in one or two cases, I'm afraid he felt the need to suggest their actions could well have unfortunate consequences if they did not stop meeting with President Kennedy.'

'And this approach has worked?'

'As I said, mostly. However, I gather, there was one woman who would not listen to Signor Gabrielli's wise words of caution, and apparently, she called in what I believe are called "bouncers" who physically threw Signor Gabrielli and his team out of the nightclub where she worked.'

'Oh my word,' said the Camerlengo, not being used to this sort of behavior. The Pope continued with his narrative.

'If you recall, Benedetto, Signor Gabrielli outlined to me a two-stage plan, and stage one involved these conversations, which, as I say, for the most part have worked extremely well. However, in the case of this nightclub women, who I am told is what's known as a stripper, in that she takes all her clothes off for the benefit of all the men watching her in the club's audience, stage one sadly proved completely unsuccessful, and Signor Gabrielli asked for my permission to move to stage two.'

'Surely you said no, Holy Father?'

'I thought long and hard about it my friend, but in the end, I felt there was no alternative. Neither she nor Kennedy had any intention whatsoever of stopping their illicit behavior, and it would have, without doubt, become public knowledge and brought both shame and disgrace on the Church. So, in all honesty, my friend, I felt I had no choice but to give my permission.'

'I hate to ask this, but what did they do?'

'I have no idea. Signor Gabrielli didn't tell me and I have never asked. He just assured me the matter had been dealt with and this stripper will not be meeting with the President ever again.'

'I'm not sure how comfortable I feel about all this, Angelo,' said the Camerlengo.

'It is not something I am proud of, but the Church was left with no choice.'

'Yes, I do see your point.'

'However,' began the Pope. 'What I never told you before was that not only did Signor Gabrielli's plan have a stage one and a stage two, it also had a stage three, and he feels it may well be necessary to start preparing for stage three.'

'I am afraid to ask, but what exactly is stage three?'
The Pope then told him.

Chapter Thirty-Two
May 1962
The White House, Washington D.C.

Evelyn closed the door behind her as she entered the Oval Office. Jack had called her in as he wanted to get his own diary as up-to-date as hers was. 'So,' he began, 'what's in the diary for the next couple of months, and I don't mean the minor stuff; I mean important meetings, travel, visits from world leaders etc.?'

'Well, Mr. President,' she replied. 'Later today, you'll be signing the Educational Television Facilities Act into law, the first time ever that Congress has provided major federal aid to public broadcasting. You then have a few minor events for the next couple of weeks leading up to your 45th birthday celebrations at Madison Square Garden.'

'That should be a great evening, although Jackie's decided not to come. She's taking the kids off somewhere for the day.'

'Is she alright, Mr. President?' Evelyn asked.

'Yes, I think she's a bit cheesed off with me as Marilyn Monroe is coming, and apparently, she's going to sing a song to me.'

'As long as that's all she's doing for you, Mr. President.'

'Now, now Evelyn. I thought we'd agreed we wouldn't talk about that side of my life, and that we'd keep strictly to business conversations.'

'I'm sorry, Mr. President, I just get upset when I see Jackie so miserable, and when you said she wasn't coming to your birthday, well, it just sort of slipped out.'

'Jackie will be here for my actual birthday on the 29th, and anyway, this Madison Square Garden do on the 19th is more of a fundraiser for the Democratic Party than a birthday party for me. So, where were we? Yes, what about June?'

'Well, at the end of June, you are doing your fifth international trip, this time to Mexico City to meet with President Adolfo Lopez Mateos.'

'OK, Evelyn, that'll do for now, and thank you.'

'Sorry about my comment earlier, Mr. President,' she said.

'Forget it, Evelyn. You're not the only person thinking it, I'm sure.'

Evelyn left the Oval Office and returned to her desk just as Bobby walked in.

'I think we have a major problem, Jack,' he announced, gently closing the door behind him to give them privacy.

'Who is it this time, Castro, Khrushchev, the Pope?'

'You're sort of right when you say the Pope. Not him personally, but I think it's to do with that lecture you got from Bishop O'Boyle last year. It's Sally Gilchrist. You must have noticed, she's just disappeared off the face of the earth. Nobody's seen her for months and I have my suspicions.'

'You think she's been warned off and done a bunk somewhere?' asked Jack.

'In all honesty, Jack, I think it's more than that. I think she's been got rid of.'

'You're joking right, Bobby? The Catholic Church doesn't go around killing people just because they don't like someone's views or their habits. You're being paranoid.'

'I don't think so. I've been checking it out, and she left the club on the Friday evening as usual to call in at the grocers and do her usual shop. Nobody's seen her since. She never made it home, she's never been back to the club, and they still have money she's owed. I got one of our "Operation Scratch" team to speak to a couple of the club's bouncers, and they said a couple of weeks before Sally disappeared, five Italian guys accosted Sally in her dressing room and told her to stop seeing you. She told them in no uncertain terms to mind their own business, and she'd do what the hell she wanted with whoever she wanted, and then she got the bouncers to throw them out of the club.'

'And you think these guys were from the Vatican? That's a bit far-fetched, don't you think, Bobby?'

'No, I don't. Think about it, Jack. First, you get a visit from the Bishop on behalf of the Vatican, and you are told, not asked, but told to stop your, as he called it, immoral behavior. Then one of the ladies you were seeing regularly, Sally, gets a visit from a bunch of guys from Italy, which just so happens to be where the Vatican is located, telling her exactly the same thing, and then soon after their visit and Sally having thrown them out, she mysteriously disappears, and has never been seen again. I'm sorry, Jack, but I think it stinks to high heaven.'

'You're worrying me now, Bobby,' said Jack, looking concerned.

'I also got one of the boys,' continued his brother, 'to check back and chat with one or two of the girls you used to see, but are no longer seeing. Gunilla von Post was warned off by Italians before she went back to Sweden, Pamela Turnure had been warned off, also by Italians, Mary Meyer was scared witless when she was warned off, and she described them as being Mediterranean sounding, and Judith Campbell has also been warned off, although she thought they were a couple of FBI agents. However, their accents were definitely Italian, she said. All the girls said the warnings came from men with Italian accents. I think the Vatican has decided that if they can't stop you, then they'll stop the women, but; just how far would they go if one of the ladies refused to listen? Well, Sally refused to listen, Jack, and she's never been seen since.'

Chapter Thirty-Three
June 1962
The Willard Hotel, Washington D.C.

The five men from the Holy Office were all gathered in Gabrielli's bedroom with the door well and truly closed and locked.

'Gentlemen,' began Gabrielli. 'The Holy Father has now authorized us to begin to discuss plans and preparations for the possible, and I say again very clearly, the possible implementation of stage three.'

'Bloody hell,' said a shocked Giuseppe. 'You mean we might...'

'Yes Giuseppe, we might, with the emphasis on might,' agreed Gabrielli.

'So, what do we do, boss?' asked Marco.

'We plan. If we do end up doing this, then every aspect has to work perfectly. Who, what, where, when, how etc.? Time, place, personnel, escape routes, who gets the blame, covering our tracks, ensuring nobody ever finds out who authorized it, etc., etc.'

'Can I just be very clear on this, boss,' asked Mario. 'I'm sorry if I'm being a bit thick, or maybe just pedantic, but are you saying we are going to start making plans to assassinate the President of the United States of America, on the orders of the Pope?'

'That is exactly what I'm saying,' confirmed Gabrielli.

'Bloody hell,' said a shocked Giuseppe.

'I agree with Giuseppe,' said Mario. 'Bloody hell.'

'That's a way off yet gentlemen, but in the meantime, we have someone else to deal with, and this one definitely has to look like a self-inflicted accident, so no guns.'

'Who are we talking about this time, boss?' asked Franco.

'A certain very well-known blonde bombshell actress who the President has been seeing rather too much of, in every sense of the word. So, gentlemen, planning, that's what we need; lots of planning. We need to ensure it looks like an accident.'

'Do we have to, boss?' pleaded Marco. 'I mean, for goodness sake, Marilyn Monroe; she's probably the most gorgeous women on the planet.'

'And that is exactly the problem,' said Gabrielli.

Marilyn Monroe's housekeeper, Eunice Murray, was staying overnight at Marilyn's home at 12305 Fifth Helena Drive in Brentwood on the evening of August 5th, 1962. Eunice woke up at 3:00 a.m. on August the 6th and somehow sensed that something was wrong. Although she saw light from under Marilyn's bedroom door, she was unable to get a response and found the door locked. Eunice then decided it was time to call for help, so she telephoned Marilyn's psychiatrist, Dr. Ralph Greenson, who arrived at the house shortly after. He broke into Marilyn's bedroom and found her dead in her bed. She was pronounced dead by her physician, Dr. Hyman Engelberg, who arrived at the house at around 3.50 am, and at 4.25 am, they notified the Los Angeles Police Department.

The Los Angeles County Coroner's Office was assisted in their investigation by psychiatrists from the Los Angeles Suicide Prevention Team, who had expert knowledge on suicide. It was estimated that Marilyn had died between 8.30 pm and 10.30 pm on the 5th of August, and the toxicology report later revealed that the cause of death was acute barbiturate poisoning. Empty bottles containing various medicines were found next to her bed. The possibility that she had accidentally overdosed was ruled out, because the dosages found in her body were several times over the lethal limit. Her doctors stated that she had been prone to severe fears and frequent depressions with abrupt and unpredictable mood changes, and had overdosed several times in the past, possibly intentionally. Due to these facts and the lack of any indication of foul play, the coroner officially classified Marilyn's death as a probable suicide.

Gabrielli heard the news on his black and white television as he sat quietly in his hotel suite, and the coroner's suicide verdict made him feel extremely gratified at a job well done. Stage two had been successful once more, and yet again, nobody had a clue.

Chapter Thirty-Four
October 1962
The White House, Washington D.C.

The previous month, Jack had an engagement at Rice University, where he spoke on the subject of the nation's plans to land human beings on the surface of the moon. During the speech, he announced his continued support for increased space expenditure, saying, 'We choose to go to the moon in this decade and do the other things, not because they are easy, but because they are hard.'

He'd long since decided that holding this particular office, that of the President of the United States, was also very hard. There was a knock at the door of the Oval Office and Evelyn entered. She was accompanied by National Security Advisor McGeorge Bundy. 'I'm sorry to interrupt whatever you are doing, Mr. President,' began Bundy, 'but I'm afraid this cannot wait.' Evelyn left the Oval and closed the door behind her. 'Late yesterday evening, Mr. President, the CIA notified the Department of State that the Soviets are installing nuclear missiles on Cuba. I have here numerous photographs taken by one of our U2's along with the CIA's analysis of the images.'

'I need some context here,' said Jack, 'so please, give me everything you know and take your time.'

Bundy began his briefing, 'In early 1962, a group of Soviet military and missile construction specialists hidden in with an agricultural delegation all flew into Havana. They obtained a meeting with the Cuban leader, Fidel Castro. The Cuban leadership had a strong expectation that the U.S. would most likely invade Cuba again, and they enthusiastically approved the idea of installing nuclear missiles in Cuba. However, according to another source, Castro objected to the missiles deployment that would have made him look like a Soviet puppet, but he was persuaded that missiles in Cuba would be an irritant to the U.S. and help the interests of the entire socialist camp.'

'Why am I only hearing about this now?' asked Jack.

'Most of this information has only just come to light, Mr. President.'

'Carry on,' said Jack. 'Also, the deployment would apparently include short-range tactical weapons, with a range of just 40 km, only usable really against naval vessels, but they felt that would provide a nuclear umbrella for attacks upon the island. By May, Khrushchev and Castro agreed to place strategic nuclear missiles secretly in Cuba. Like Castro, Khrushchev felt that a U.S. invasion of Cuba was imminent and that to lose Cuba would do great harm to the communists, especially in Latin America. He said he wanted to confront the Americans with more than words, and the logical answer was missiles.'

'I presume this information has come from human intelligence?' asked Jack.

'Yes, Mr. President, the CIA has numerous agents operating inside Cuba. From the very beginning, the Soviets' operation entailed elaborate denial and deception, which they apparently call "*maskirovka*". All the planning and preparation for transporting and deploying the missiles on Cuba were carried out in the utmost secrecy, with only a very few people being told the exact nature of the mission. Even the troops detailed for the mission were given misdirection by being told that they were headed for a cold region and being outfitted with ski boots, fleece-lined parkas, and other winter equipment.'

'Crafty bastards,' muttered Jack. 'Anyway, specialists in missile construction under the guise of machine operators, irrigation specialists, and agricultural specialists arrived in July. A total of 43,000 foreign troops would ultimately be brought in. Marshal Sergei Biryuzov, chief of the Soviet

Rocket Forces, led a survey team that visited Cuba. He told Khrushchev that the missiles would be concealed and camouflaged by palm trees.'

'Tell me about the actual missiles,' said Jack. 'How far can they actually reach?'

'They have two types on Cuba. SS-4 SANDAL's and SS-5 SKEANS. They are both carrying single warheads with a yield of between 1.0 and 2.3 Mt. The SS-4's have a range of roughly 1,250 miles, but the SS-5's can reach 2,300 miles. In other words, Mr. President, those missiles can take out Washington D.C. and New York.'

'You're sure of this?' asked Jack.

'One hundred percent, Mr. President. A lot of this all stems from when Congress approved September's Joint Resolution 230. We saw it as simply expressing our resolve to prevent the creation of a military establishment on Cuba, externally supported by the Soviets. The Cuban leadership, however, saw it as an act of aggression, particularly when on the same day, the U.S. announced a major military exercise in the Caribbean. Cuba immediately denounced the exercises as a deliberate provocation and proof that the U.S. was planning to invade Cuba.'

'They're bloody paranoid,' mused Jack, smiling to himself.

'As I was saying, Mr. President, the Soviet leadership believed, based on its perception of your personal lack of confidence during the Bay of Pigs Invasion, that you would avoid confrontation and accept the missiles as a *fait accompli*.'

'Like hell. There's no way I'll accept Soviet nuclear missiles that close to the United States, and definitely not if they can reach our major cities.'

'If you remember, Mr. President, back on September the 11th, the Soviet Union publicly warned that a U.S. attack on Cuba or on Soviet ships that were carrying supplies to the island would mean war. The Soviets then continued the Maskirovka program to conceal their actions in Cuba. They have repeatedly denied that the weapons being brought into Cuba were offensive in nature, and as you no doubt remember, on October 17th, Soviet embassy official Georgy Bolshakov brought you a personal message from Khrushchev reassuring you that under no circumstances would surface-to-surface missiles be sent to Cuba. I'm sorry, Mr. President. That was an outright lie.'

Jack got up from behind his desk and started pacing round the Oval Office, obviously deep in thought. The National Security Advisor remained in his seat and kept quiet, leaving Jack to his thought.

'Carry on, Mr. Bundy, and tell me how many of these missiles are there on Cuba?'

'The planned arsenal was forty launchers, Mr. President. The missiles in Cuba will allow the Soviets to target effectively most of the Continental U.S. The CIA and the NSA have received five reports, all of which bothered the analysts. They described large trucks passing through towns at night that were carrying very long canvas-covered cylindrical objects that could not make turns through towns without backing up and maneuvering. We know for a fact that Soviet defensive missiles could turn without maneuvering, so it was reasoned these must be strike missiles. These reports could not be satisfactorily dismissed.'

'Who actually obtained these photographs?' Jack asked, looking at several prints.

'Major Richard Heyser, Mr. President. His was the first U-2 flight to obtain definite photographic evidence of the missiles on October 14, when his U-2 took 928 pictures on a path selected by DIA analysts, capturing images of what turned out to be an SS-4 construction site at San Cristóbal, Pinar del Río Province in western Cuba. On October 15th, the CIA's National Photographic Interpretation Centre reviewed the U-2 photographs and identified objects that they interpreted as medium range ballistic missiles. The identification was made, in part, on the strength of reporting provided by Oleg Penkovsky, who you may recall is a double agent in the GRU working for both the CIA and MI6.'

'Thank you, Mr. Bundy. You know I've always thought the role of the National Security Advisor must be one of the most difficult jobs in American government, and you have proved today that you are doing an excellent job.'

'Thank you, Mr. President.'

Later that day, at 6:30 pm, Jack convened a meeting of the nine members of the National Security Council and five other key advisors, in a group he formally named the Executive Committee of the National Security Council. Without informing the members of the committee, Jack tape-recorded all of their proceedings, and Sheldon M. Stern, head of the Kennedy library later transcribed some of them. The U.S., at that stage, had no plan in place because its intelligence had been convinced that the Soviets would never install nuclear missiles in Cuba. The committee quickly discussed several possible courses of action.

Their first option was to do nothing. Vulnerability to Soviet missiles was not new. Another possibility was to try diplomacy, and use diplomatic pressure to get the Soviet Union to remove the missiles. Then there was the secret approach; offer Castro the choice of splitting with the Russians or being invaded. The heavy option was, of course, the full force invasion of Cuba and the overthrow of Castro. Another possibility they discussed was getting the U.S. Air Force to attack all known missile sites. Finally, there was the suggestion of Blockade; use the U.S. Navy to block any missiles from arriving in Cuba. The Joint Chiefs of Staff unanimously agreed that a full-scale attack and invasion was the only solution. They believed that the Soviets would not attempt to stop the U.S. from conquering Cuba. Jack, however, was skeptical.

'They, no more than we,' he said, 'can let these things go by without us or them doing something to respond. They can't, after all their statements, permit us to take out their missiles, kill a lot of Russians, and then do nothing. Even if they don't take action in Cuba, they certainly will in Berlin.'

Jack concluded that attacking Cuba by air would signal the Soviets to presume a clear line to conquer Berlin. Jack also believed that U.S. allies would think of the country as trigger-happy cowboys who lost Berlin because they could not peacefully resolve the Cuban situation. Jack agreed with the committee that the missiles would definitely affect the political balance. He'd explicitly promised the American people less than a month before the crisis that 'If Cuba should possess a capacity to carry out offensive actions against the United States... the United States would act.' Also, Jack felt, credibility among U.S. allies and people would be damaged if the Soviet Union appeared to redress the strategic balance by placing missiles in Cuba.

On October 22, at 7:00 pm, Jack delivered a nationwide televised address on all of the major networks announcing the discovery of the missiles. He said, 'It shall be the policy of this nation to regard any nuclear missile launched from Cuba against any nation in the Western Hemisphere as an attack by the Soviet Union on the United States, requiring a full retaliatory response upon the Soviet Union. To halt this offensive build up, a strict quarantine on all offensive military equipment under shipment to Cuba is being initiated. All ships of any kind bound for Cuba, from whatever nation or port, will, if found to contain cargoes of offensive weapons, be turned back. This quarantine will be extended, if needed, to other types of cargo and carriers. We are not, at this time, however, denying the necessities of life as the Soviets attempted to do in their Berlin blockade of 1948.'

While Jack was talking to the nation, a directive went out to all U.S. forces worldwide, placing them all on DEFCON 3. The heavy cruiser USS Newport News was designated flagship for the blockade, with USS Leary as Newport News' destroyer escort. The crisis was continuing unabated, and in the evening of October 24, the Soviet news agency TASS broadcast a telegram from Khrushchev to Kennedy in which Khrushchev warned that the United States' outright piracy would lead to war.' However, that was followed at 9:24 pm by a telegram from Khrushchev to Kennedy, which was received at 10:52 pm. Khrushchev stated, 'If you weigh the present situation with a cool head without giving way to passion, you will understand that the Soviet Union cannot afford not to decline the despotic demands of the USA,' and that the Soviet Union views the blockade as "an act of aggression" and their ships will be instructed to ignore it.

In response, Jack requested an emergency meeting of the United Nations Security Council on October 25. U.S. Ambassador to the United Nations, Adlai Stevenson, confronted Soviet Ambassador, Valerian Zorin, in an emergency meeting of the Security Council, challenging him to admit the existence of the missiles. Ambassador Zorin refused to answer. The next day at 10:00 pm, the U.S. raised the readiness level of SAC forces to DEFCON 2. For the only confirmed time in US history, B-52 bombers went on continuous airborne alert, and B-47 medium bombers were dispersed to various military and civilian airfields and made ready to take off, fully equipped, on 15 minutes' notice. One eighth of SAC's 1,436 bombers were on airborne alert, and some 145 intercontinental ballistic missiles stood on ready alert, some of which targeted Cuba. Air Defence Command redeployed 161 nuclear-armed interceptors to 16 dispersal fields within nine hours, with one-third maintaining 15-minute alert status. 23 nuclear-armed B-52s were sent to orbit points within striking distance of the Soviet Union so that it would believe that the U.S. was serious. The Russians didn't make any move. They did not increase their alert, they did not increase any flights, or their air defense posture. They didn't do a thing; they froze in place. On October 25 at 1.45 am, Jack responded to Khrushchev's telegram by stating that the U.S. was forced into action after receiving repeated assurances that no offensive missiles were being placed in Cuba, and when the assurances proved to be false, the deployment required the responses he had announced. Jack also said that he 'hoped your government will take necessary action to permit a restoration of the earlier situation.'

On Saturday, October 27, after much deliberation between the Soviet Union and Jack's cabinet, Jack secretly agreed to remove all the missiles set in Turkey and possibly those in southern Italy. The Turkish-based missiles would definitely be removed, Jack promised, in exchange for Khrushchev removing all missiles in Cuba. Khrushchev knew he was losing control. Jack had been told in early 1961 that a nuclear war would likely kill a third of humanity, with most or all of those deaths concentrated in the U.S., the USSR, Europe and China. Khrushchev had more than likely received similar reports from his military. With this background, when Khrushchev heard Jack's threats relayed by Robert Kennedy to Soviet Ambassador Dobrynin, he immediately drafted his acceptance of Jack's latest terms from his dacha without involving the Politburo, as he had previously, and had them immediately broadcasts over Radio Moscow, which he believed the U.S. would hear. In that broadcast, at 9.00 am on October 28, Khrushchev stated that 'the Soviet government, in addition to previously issued instructions on the cessation of further work at the building sites for the weapons, has issued a new order for the dismantling of the weapons which you describe as "offensive" and their crating and return to the Soviet Union.' What had become known around the world as the Cuban Missile Crisis was now over, and the threatened nuclear war had been averted.

Chapter Thirty-Five
November 1962
The Willard Hotel, Washington D.C.

'OK gentlemen, let's review what we have agreed on,' began
Gabrielli. 'We've discussed numerous possible options for
the assassination including bombs, gas, drugs etc., but we all
feel high-powered hunting rifles are the only real way of
ensuring the job is done, and done properly, but it also gives
us the best escape possibilities. Franco here, is the only
member of the team with the necessary expertise and the right
amount of skill in this area, and he feels we'll need three
shooters in total, and all three shooting from different angles
to guarantee one hundred percent success. That means we
need to recruit two more people as soon as possible.'

'Where the hell do we find specialist assassins?' asked
Giuseppe.

'Back in Italy, or more accurately; Sicily.'

'Of course,' smiled Mario, 'the family.'

'Have we settled upon when and where yet?' asked
Marco.

'There are several options at this stage,' answered
Gabrielli. 'Kennedy is going to Costa Rica in March and that
could offer possibilities. Then he'll be in West Berlin at the
end of June, and if we can be ready in time, that is my
preferred option at this stage.'

'Why, boss?' asked Giuseppe.

'Because it will be blamed on the East Germans, and
everybody will believe it. They know the Soviets and
everyone associated with communism can't stand Kennedy,
especially since they were humiliated when they had to back

down over the Cuban Missile Crisis. But if not West Berlin, there are still other possibilities. Would you believe he has an audience with the Holy Father scheduled for early July, and then he's dedicating some dam in the middle of California? Lastly, he'll be in Dallas at the end of November. From what we know so far, he'll be travelling in an open car, and that should present opportunities.'

'So, what's your first choice, boss?' asked Franco.

'Oh, without doubt, West Berlin at the end of June, but sadly, I fear that may be too early. We may not be ready in time.'

Chapter Thirty-Six
January 1963
The Vatican, Rome, Italy

'Benedetto,' began the Pope, sitting in a comfortable armchair in his private quarters, 'you are not only my Camerlengo, you are also my dear and closest friend, and I now tell you this as my friend. As you know, for nearly eight months now, I have been from time-to-time suffering from occasional stomach hemorrhages. Having seen my physician again yesterday, I feel it is now time you knew this, but I beg you, please keep it to yourself for the time being. Last September, the 23rd to be exact, I saw him in a private consultation and after several tests, I was diagnosed with stomach cancer. It is sadly untreatable and I am afraid, terminal. The diagnosis, which I implore you must be kept from the public, will, I understand, mean reducing my public appearances, as I am told I will start looking very pale and drawn quite soon, so I ask you to keep my diary free as much as you can during my last few months.'

'Is there anything I can do, Angelo, for you personally I mean, not as the Pope?'

'They are one and the same person, my dear Benedetto. I just need you to promise me that the work I have started will continue. I have tried to do my best for the Church and hopefully, I have been a good Pope. In fact, it would be nice to be remembered as a good Pope.'

'I must admit,' said the Camerlengo, 'Good Pope John has a nice ring to it.'

'As you know, as much as I totally abhor his private behavior, Kennedy is still the President of the United States, and so I felt it my duty to offer to mediate between him and the Soviet leader Nikita Khrushchev during the recent Cuban Missile Crisis. My offer was sadly, not taken up by either side, but at least I offered.'

'What are you going to do about Kennedy, and what about Gabrielli?'

'Signor Gabrielli has my full confidence in this matter, and he assures me he has the situation well in hand. I am now happy to leave the matter entirely with him. I am sure he will do what is best for the Church. My successor, whoever that may be, need not know about any of this, because hopefully the American President will, in the meantime, have changed his ways, and this will all have been irrelevant.'

'But what if he doesn't?' asked the Camerlengo.

'Then it is in God's hands, and those of Signor Gabrielli.'

Chapter Thirty-Seven
March 1963
The Willard Hotel, Washington D.C.

'Gentlemen,' began Gabrielli. 'I have managed to secure the services of several of our colleagues from various families in Sicily. They do not know what the mission is at this stage, and for the time being, it must remain that way, but they have all agreed to do whatever is required of them. The target must never be mentioned or identified to any of them until I say the word. The four of you I trust, but I do not know the six joining us as well as I know you.'

'When do they arrive, boss?' asked Marco.

'Not for another two weeks, and that gives us time to finalize our plans.'

'Are we still looking at West Berlin?' asked Franco.

'If possible, but time is running short. You and I, Franco, will fly to Germany tomorrow, and see if we can identify enough locations from which the deed can be done. If we can, then West Berlin it is. If not, then I think we will have to switch to Dallas.'

Five days later, Gabrielli and Franco were back at the Willard Hotel.

'How did it go boss?' asked Giuseppe.

'A complete washout. There's no way we could find three different locations, and to be frank, it would be hard enough finding even one that would give us a clear shot.'

'Security in West Berlin is totally over-the-top crazy,' said Franco. 'You can't move anywhere without someone watching you. Getting high-powered rifles in would be extremely difficult, and as for finding three locations, well, it was difficult enough finding one in the last few days, but when Kennedy is there, it will be ten times worse.'

'Franco's right,' said Gabrielli. 'Forget West Berlin. It's going to be Dallas.'

Chapter Thirty-Eight
May 1963
The Vatican, Rome, Italy

On the 25th of May, 1963, Pope John XXIII suffered another hemorrhage and required several blood transfusions, but the cancer had now perforated the stomach wall, and peritonitis soon set in. The doctors conferred in a decision regarding this matter and John XXIII's aide Loris F. Capovilla broke the news to him saying that the cancer had done its work and nothing could be done for him. Around this time, his remaining siblings arrived to be with him. By the 31st of May, it had become clear that the cancer had overcome the resistance of John XXIII – it had left him confined to his bed.

At 11 am, Petrus Canisius Van Lierde as Papal Sacristan was at the bedside of the dying Pope, ready to anoint him. The pope began to speak for the very last time. 'I had the great grace to be born into a Christian family, modest and poor, but with the fear of the Lord. My time on earth is drawing to a close.'

Pope John XXIII died peacefully of peritonitis caused by a perforated stomach at 19.49 local time on the 3rd of June, 1963 at the age of 81, ending a historic pontificate of four years and seven months. He died just as a Mass for him finished in Saint Peter's Square below, celebrated by Luigi Traglia. After he died, his brow was ritually tapped to see if he was dead, and those with him in the room said prayers. The room was then illuminated, informing the people of what had happened. He was buried on the 6th of June in the Vatican grottos. The papal conclave, which met from the 19th to the

21st of June, in the Sistine Chapel in Vatican City, was the largest ever assembled. There were 82 cardinal electors eligible to participate. The only two who did not were Cardinal József Mindszenty, who refused to leave the U.S. Legation in Budapest, where he had lived since 1956, unless the Hungarian government met his demands for religious freedom in Hungary. The other was Cardinal Carlos María de la Torre of Quito, Ecuador, who was 89 years old and could not make the journey because he had suffered a stroke the previous December and was bedridden with thrombosis. Of the eighty cardinals who did participate, eight had been elevated by Pope Pius XI, twenty-seven by Pius XII, and the remainder by John XXIII. Each cardinal elector was allowed one aide.

Under the latest rules, election required the votes of two-thirds of those voting, in this case 54. No ballots were taken on the first day, and there was just a lot of discussion as to who the Cardinals felt was the most likely "frontrunners" to succeed Pope John XXIII. From these discussions, several names emerged. Over the following days, there were indeed ballots, two each morning and two each afternoon. There had been confusion at the last conclave in 1958 over the color of the smoke used to indicate whether a pope had been elected, so the smoke would now be supplemented with electric lights.

The results of the first four ballots were signaled with black smoke on the 20th of June at 11:54 am and 5:47 pm.

Some reform-minded cardinals it was later reported had initially voted apparently for Cardinal Leo Joseph Suenens of Mechelen-Brussels and Cardinal Franz König of Vienna in order to make the point that the Pope did not have to be an Italian. Other reports said that many conservative cardinals attempted to block Cardinal Montini's election in the early balloting. Due to the apparent deadlock, Cardinal Montini proposed to withdraw himself from being considered but was silenced by Cardinal Giovanni Urbani, the Patriarch of Venice. Another cardinal, Gustavo Testa, an old friend of Pope John XXIII, lost his temper in the Chapel and demanded that the intransigents stop impeding Cardinal Montini's path.

By the fourth ballot on the 20th of June, according to Time Magazine, Cardinal Montini needed only four additional votes to obtain the required number of votes. He was elected on the fifth ballot on the morning of the 21st of June. When asked by Eugène Tisserant if he accepted his election, Cardinal Montini replied, 'I accept, in the name of the Lord.' He chose to be known as Pope Paul VI.

At 11:22 am, white smoke rose from the chimney of the Sistine Chapel, signifying the election of a new pope, and as usual, the crowds in St. Peter's Square were ecstatic. Alfredo Ottaviani, in his capacity as the senior Cardinal Deacon, announced Cardinal Montini's election in Latin. Before Ottaviani had even finished saying Montini's name, the crowd beneath the balcony of St. Peter's Basilica erupted into applause. Pope Paul VI appeared on the balcony shortly afterwards to give his first blessing. On this occasion, Paul VI chose not to give the traditional Urbi et Orbi blessing, but instead gave the much shorter episcopal blessing; his first Apostolic Blessing.

Chapter Thirty-Nine
June 1963
The Willard Hotel, Washington D.C.

Gabrielli and his four associates sat watching the television news about the election of the new Pope. Gabrielli was one of the few who had known Pope John XXIII was dying, as he'd been informed personally during one of their updates two months earlier.

'Does this affect us and what we are doing?' asked Mario.

'Not at all,' replied Gabrielli. 'Pope John left the final decision on this to me, and he instructed me that if the President changed his ways, then we should respond in kind by changing our plans. However, for the sake of the Church, if the President didn't stop his immoral behavior then it was up to me to decide if, when and how to stop it.'

'That's one hell of a big decision, boss,' commented Giuseppe.

'It goes with the territory, as they say,' replied Gabrielli. 'Look, my friends, I'm sure you all agree; Kennedy is never going to give up his womanizing. To be perfectly honest, I don't think he'd know how to even if he tried. So, in reality, we have no choice to make. We continue to make plans for Dallas.'

Chapter Forty
June 1963
West Berlin, Germany

At the end of World War II, the victorious Allied powers had divided Germany into four zones. Three of those, controlled by the United States, the United Kingdom and France, respectively, became democratic West Germany, whereas the one controlled by the Soviet Union became communist East Germany. Berlin, the former capital, was similarly split despite being located squarely within East Germany's borders; a situation that rankled with the Soviet Union. In June 1948, the USSR cut off all land and water routes between West Berlin and the rest of West Germany in an attempt to gain control over the city. But the United States and its allies were able to overcome this eleven-month blockade by airlifting-in over 2.3 million tons of food and supplies. Berlin remained a point of contention between the United States and the Soviet Union when John Fitzgerald Kennedy took office in January 1961. At a summit that June in Austria, Soviet leader Nikita Khrushchev threatened the sovereignty of West Berlin and ratcheted up the rhetoric, warning that it was "up to the U.S. to decide whether there will be war or peace" between the two nations and insisting that as the Cold War heated up "force will be met by force". Khrushchev then approved the construction of the Berlin Wall in order to prevent any more East Germans from fleeing to the West, with an estimated 3.5 million having already done so. Barbed wire went up on August 13, 1961; concrete blocks later replaced it. More turmoil came in October, when Soviet and U.S. tanks rolled to within a few hundred feet of each other at

Checkpoint Charlie, the crossing point for diplomats and other non-Germans. The sixteen-hour standoff ended without any shots being fired. On June 23, 1963, President Kennedy returned to Europe for the first time since sparring with Khrushchev in Austria. He visited Bonn, Cologne and Frankfurt in West Germany, where big crowds chanted his name and waved U.S. flags, before flying into West Berlin on the morning of June the 26th. On the way over, he showed General James H. Polk, the U.S. commandant in Berlin, a draft of the speech he planned to give later that day.

'I'm sorry, but this is terrible Mr. President,' Polk said. Jack agreed with him and began working out a more forceful version in his head as he toured Checkpoint Charlie and other locations around the city. He also inserted a little German, which he wrote phonetically on note cards. Meanwhile, at least 120,000 West Berliners, some estimates placed the total as high as 450,000, had gathered in the plaza outside city hall to hear the President speak. Early in his address, the foreign language-challenged president broke out four German words he had been practicing for several days. 'Two thousand years ago, the proudest boast was "*civis Romanus sum*",' Jack said. 'Today, in the world of freedom, the proudest boast is "*Ich bin ein Berliner*".'

Jack then went on to lambaste the failures of communism, saying anyone who thought it was the way of the future should come to Berlin. 'Freedom has many difficulties and democracy is not perfect, but we have never had to put a wall up to keep our people in,' Jack stated. After praising the people of West Berlin for being at the front lines of the Cold War, he finished up by repeating his soon-to-be famous phrase. 'All free men, wherever they may live, are citizens of Berlin, and, therefore, as a free man, I take pride in the words '*Ich bin ein Berliner*!' Jack exclaimed. The entire Berlin speech had only lasted nine minutes, but without doubt, it was the best-received speech Jack ever gave. The President then gave another address later at the Free University of Berlin before flying to Ireland that evening. 'We'll never have another day like this one' Jack said. 'Not as long as we live.

Gabrielli leaned forward and turned off the television. He sent Mario off to gather everybody into his room, and they all sat down, on chairs, on the bed, or on the floor. There were now eleven of them in his hotel suite; Gabrielli himself, his four original associates; Mario, Marco, Franco and Giuseppe, plus the six new faces from Sicily. Gabrielli already knew Bernardo Bartelli as he too was from Palermo, and he was also a distant cousin of Gabrielli's. Bernardo would be the second gunman and was a very experienced assassin having worked exclusively for the mafia until now. The third gunman was a man Gabrielli had never met, but he'd definitely heard of him as Paolo Frascatti was a legend on the island of Sicily. The other four men were Jacques, Rafael, Theodore and Salvador.

'Gentlemen, we have all been together now for two days, and it is now time to outline the plan, and allocate a series of tasks. Every task I decide to give you is just as important as any other, and so you will undertake every task given to you with honesty and determination to succeed. I will accept nothing less. You men have been specifically chosen as you are all tenacious hard workers and excellent in your own chosen fields. The objective is very simple, and that is to shoot the target in the head using crossfire, and thus, ensuring he is well and truly dead.'

'May we know who the target is?' asked Rafael.

'I was originally intending to keep the target a mystery until nearer the time, but I think I need to know now if any of you are uncertain about undertaking this task and seeing it through to the end. It will also be helpful for each of you if you all know the target when it comes to discussions about planning and the simple logistics.'

'So who is the target?' repeated Rafael.

'Gentlemen, we are going to assassinate the President of the United States.'

Chapter Forty-One
July, 1963
The White House, Washington D.C.

Jack was preparing to fly off yet again. This time to Naples in Italy, and then on to Rome. Tomorrow, Jack was scheduled to have an audience with the newly elected Pope Paul VI at the Apostolic Palace in Vatican City. Jack was desperately hoping this new Pope was not going to challenge him about his private life, at least, not during this visit. When Air Force One landed at Rome's Fiumicino on July 1, 1963, there were only a few people there to welcome him. The welcome was subdued because of the recent event which had shaken the country; the death of Pope John XXIII. Because of the funeral of Pope John, and the recent coronation of the new pontiff, Giovanni Battista Cardinal Montini of Milan (now known as Pope Paul VI), Jack had offered to cancel the trip to Italy altogether. The Italian government, however, had looked forward to welcoming President Kennedy. They insisted that it was fine and he should still come. Originally, Jack had planned just to visit West Germany in an effort to bolster that country's allegiance to the West and to the NATO alliance, but as so often happens with the planning of presidential foreign trips, concerns and objections were raised about the itinerary. Other allies suddenly needed to be recognized and encouraged, and before long, other nations were added to the trip. What started out as a simple visit to a NATO ally had, before he knew it, been turned into a full-blown tour, and in addition to West Germany, Italy, Britain, and Ireland had now been added.

On Air Force One, Jack was still chatting. 'I'm worried Dean,' he said to Secretary of State Dean Rusk. 'How should the first-ever Catholic president of the United States handle the delicate matter of an audience with the Pope? If I adhere to traditional practice, in which all Catholics when presented to the Pope, kneel, grasp the Pope's right hand, and kiss the papal ring, I'll upset every non-Catholic in the country. But if I don't, then I'll upset every Catholic in the country.'

'And you're asking me, Mr. President?'

'Sure, Dean. You have an opinion, don't you?'

'I do, but I'm not sure you'll want to hear it, Mr. President.'

'Try me, Dean. I promise, whatever you say, you won't be sacked,' laughed Jack.

'In that case,' began the Secretary of State, 'you are the undisputed leader of the most powerful nation on the planet and the free world, and you were elected by the people for that specific purpose. As for the Pope? Well, as far as I'm concerned, he's just a glorified vicar in a posh white frock, chosen by all his mates in their posh red frocks. Sorry, Mr. President, but you did ask.'

Jack wasn't annoyed, and in fact, he was laughing. 'You know, Dean, my father's got a framed copy on his wall of a cartoon that had been published in a Baptist periodical during the 1960 campaign. Under the caption "Big John and Little John", it showed Pope John XXIII sitting on his throne with his hand on my head, bidding me to "be sure to do what Poppa tells you". He calls it a reality check as to the true nature of the Catholic Church.'

'I called my old friend, the archbishop of Boston, Richard Cardinal Cushing, for some advice about the Vatican aspect of the trip,' said the Secretary of State. 'He told me to stay away from Rome until all the ceremonies for the new Pope are concluded. He said to me, "It's the biggest day of the man's life and you don't want to take the attention away from him". So,' continued the Secretary, 'that's why Air Force One has been diverted to Milan and

Lake Como. Pope Paul's coronation is on Sunday; we were due to land in Rome on Sunday.'

'Exactly,' replied Jack. 'He now gets his day in the spotlight and we arrive in Rome the following day. Everybody's happy.'

'But what about the kneeling and kissing the ring bit, Mr. President? The vast majority of Americans will see it as you putting the Pope above the office of the President. In other words, making the Presidency inferior to the Church. If I can be totally pragmatic, Mr. President, the American people all have a vote; Catholics around the world don't.'

'You've got an extremely good point there, Dean,' mused Jack 'Perhaps I'll meet him halfway.' Sampling the infamous Roman traffic in a convertible limousine, Roman women, eager for their chance to see the American President, ran right out into the streets from the beauty parlors, with towels on their shoulders and curlers in their hair. Many hoped to get close enough to touch his car, or more hopefully, to touch Jack himself. The new Pope was also eager to meet the American President as well, as he'd personally been acquainted with various members of the Kennedy family going right back to 1939 when, as a member of the Vatican Secretariat of State, he had met them when they attended the coronation of Pope Pius XII in 1939. At that time, Jack's father, Joseph P. Kennedy, was FDR's ambassador to Great Britain, and he was regarded as a prominent American Catholic.

The moment eventually came, amid the crush of photographers and members of the press, and the Pope and the President simply shook hands. Obviously pleased and delighted, Paul VI, the new pope, resplendent in his red mozzetta and stole, offered his hand to Jack, who was dressed in a plain blue business suit and tie. Jack, obviously realizing the importance of this moment, gave a slight nod of his head in the pontiff's direction and they both shook hands solemnly. Pope Paul VI spoke English fluently, and so no interpreter was necessary. Accompanying Jack for his audience with the Pope were his sister, Jean Kennedy

Smith, Secretary of State Dean Rusk, the chief of protocol Angier Biddle Duke, presidential speechwriter and aide Theodore Sorensen, press secretary Pierre Salinger and the two members of what had become known as JFK's Irish mafia, David F. Powers and Kenneth P. O'Donnell.

Chapter Forty-Two
August 1963
The Willard Hotel, Washington D.C.

With the arrival of the six extra bodies from Sicily, Gabrielli had decided to move out of his original small suite, comfortable though it was, and instead, he'd taken over the largest suite in the hotel. He felt he had no choice as he needed the additional space for meetings with a team of eleven people to look after. He tried and eventually succeeded in convincing himself that taking the biggest suite in the hotel for himself was simply the responsible thing to do.

'Tomorrow,' he began, 'we are all flying to Dallas. Franco, Bernardo and Paolo will be with me, and we'll be looking for suitable locations from which we can get triangulated targeting. I think that's what you called it, Franco? You explain; it's your specialty, not mine.'

'Triangulated targeting,' began Franco, explaining to everyone, 'means getting your target in a central position between three different shooters. That way it doesn't matter if the target moves away from one shooter, as in doing so he's automatically moving closer to another shooter. We know exactly where the target will be at any given moment due to the exact route being made public, so we just have to find three positions from which to shoot from. We know Kennedy will be travelling by car, and that means he's a moving target, which, of course, makes any shot more difficult. But we also know that it's an open-topped car and with triangulated targeting, we'll be sure at least one of us will hit him.'

'Head or body shots, Franco?' asked Bernardo.

'Head, without doubt. I know body shots are easier as there's a bigger area to aim for, but there's a far greater risk of merely injuring him or perhaps just wounding him, but not actually killing him. A couple of well-placed bullets in the head means he'll be dead. End of story, end of JFK.'

'OK,' said Gabrielli. 'So that's what the four of us will be doing tomorrow. Now, Mario, can you please take Theodore and Salvador with you tomorrow when you meet this guy you found that really hates Kennedy. What's his name again?'

'A guy called Lee Harvey Oswald,' replied Mario. 'He's American, an ex-Marine, but he's also a Marxist and he loves the Soviets. He was honorably discharged from the Marine Corps in 1959, and then the creep defected to the Soviet Union back in October of that same year. He lived in the Belarusian city of Minsk until June 1962, when he decided to return to the United States with his new Russian wife, a woman called Marina. The two of them eventually settled in Dallas, but despite living here, he hates America, he hates Kennedy and everything he stands for.'

'Will he do what we want?' asked Gabrielli.

'I've met with him twice now, boss, and he thinks we are from the CIA, and that he's been recruited by them. We'll get him to fire a few shots at the President's car, but it doesn't really matter if he hits anything or not, and then we'll make sure the Dallas cops are tipped off where to find him, and where to find his rifle. He'll make the ideal patsy.'

'Make sure he's one hundred percent on board,' said Gabrielli. 'Tell him one of our CIA guys will stay with him while he does the shooting if that will help, and then tell him you'll help him with his escape. Lead him off somewhere and get him to sit tight while you notify the cops. Oh, and make sure he leaves the rifle behind.'

'Will do boss,' replied Mario. 'Jacques, you're our scrounger-in-chief, and we're going to need four Dallas police uniforms on the day. Full kit, with belts, caps, the lot. Can you get them from theatrical costumiers or somewhere?'

'No need, boss,' he replied. 'I'll just nick four complete uniforms. Police in every city always have a contract with local dry cleaners. I'll find out which one, and break in there overnight. Can you let me know what sizes we'll need?'

'Best you measure everyone up yourself, Jacques, just to be on the safe side.'

'I'll do that straight after your briefing, boss.'

'Good man,' said Gabrielli. 'Now Rafael, I need you to go and spend a lot of someone else's money.'

'Oh, I think I can do that boss quite easily, boss. I love spending money, especially if it's someone else's.'

'Talk to Franco, Bernardo and Paolo and find out the exact make and model of rifles they'll need, which telescopic sights, do they need tripods, and if so, what size etc., etc., and then go and buy exactly what they need. I'll supply you with all the necessary cash, but this is important. Whatever you do, don't buy any two items in the same shop. Spread your purchases around, and drive to other cities if you need to but stay within Texas. I don't want you crossing any state lines with weapons in the boot, especially high-powered rifles with telescopic sights.'

'Will do, boss,' said Rafael, 'but it might take me a couple of days.'

'No problem; take as long as you need,' replied Gabrielli. 'Now Giuseppe, I want you and Marco to set up some sort of communication link between us all on the day, so that I can communicate with everyone and control the entire operation. I assume such things exist?'

'Yes, they do boss, but they are not easy to get hold of as they're mostly intended for military use. HT-1E walkie-talkie sets are the best, and they are ideally what we need. They're currently being manufactured for use in the Vietnam War. They're fairly basic radios designed to be simple and robust, and they were originally supplied to the locals so that they could keep the USA informed about Viet Cong movements.'

'Are they large?' asked Gabrielli.

'Well, they are about 12 inches tall,' replied Giuseppe, 'and they are powered by eight D-size 12-volt batteries. They have an external aerial that is only one-foot long when it's retracted, but the aerial is nearly six-foot when it's extended.

The radio's cases are really strong and they are made from extruded aluminum, with squelch, volume controls and external connectors for the aerial, the battery and earphones to be attached. They'll be perfect for the job, and I'm sure we can filch some from a military base somewhere, but the aerials are very visible, so we'll all need to be somewhere invisible to the public, and more importantly, to the cops.'

'That's exactly why we're heading to Dallas in the morning,' responded Gabrielli. 'To find lots of nice secretive places from where we can shoot and kill the President.'

Chapter Forty-Three
August 1963
White Plaza Hotel, Dallas, Texas

They were all staying in the White Plaza hotel, formally the Dallas Hilton, but this was one of the four hotels Conrad Hilton lost during the great depression. A man named George Loudermilk had bought the property, and then he handed over the running of it to a well-known Texas hotel proprietor named A. C. White. He decided the former Dallas Hilton badly needed updating, so he spent a lot of money on it, upgrading all the rooms, redecorating etc. When everything was finally finished, he changed the name and launched it as the White Plaza. Gabrielli, Franco, Bernardo, Giuseppe and Paolo were talking in Gabrielli's suite about the route Kennedy's motorcade was going to take. JFK's visit to Dallas had been talked about in all the local magazines and newspapers, and it had even been mentioned on several television reports from Dallas. The proposed route was even shown on a full-page map in one of the Dallas daily newspapers. Gabrielli had bought a copy of the newspaper and pinned the map to the wall in his hotel suite. Alongside it, he'd also pinned up a large-scale map of Dallas and the surrounding area that he'd bought locally.

'OK, all of you,' Gabrielli began. 'Use your notebooks and write down what I'm going to run through. I don't want to have to keep repeating myself.'

'Will do, boss,' muttered Giuseppe. Gabrielli smiled; he really liked Giuseppe.

'Firstly, the President and Mrs. Kennedy's aircraft will land here at Dallas Love Field,' he said, pointing at the map.

'They'll then proceed to Dallas city in a motorcade, with JFK in the second car; the Presidential Limo. Secondly, that car will be a 1961 open-top four-door Lincoln Convertible. Thank you, God, for inventing open-top convertible cars. It will make our task ten times easier. Thirdly. The route they've planned means JFK's car will approach the intersection of Houston Street and Elm Street just here.' Gabrielli was using a long stick of wooden doweling to point out the route on the map pinned to his wall, just like his old teacher used to do when he was a pupil at his old school in Sicily. 'This means that when they reach the extreme west end of Main Street, the motorcade will turn right on Houston Street and then proceed north for one block in order to make a left turn just here on Elm Street. At this point, the motorcade and, in particular, the Limo will have to slow right down, and I think that's when we strike.'

'So that will be the point for the center of triangulation boss?' asked Franco.

'Exactly,' Gabrielli replied. 'Well, at least somewhere in this stretch of road. Now, Franco, Bernardo, Paolo and I will be heading there later this morning to start looking for the most suitable places for our three guns to shoot from, and we'll also need to find somewhere for Oswald to shoot from. As for the rest of the team? Well, Giuseppe, you've got a list of everyone's various tasks, so make a start on them, and we'll all meet back here at 6.00 pm this evening for an update.'

They all headed into Dallas and split into their various groups, each with their own tasks. Gabrielli and his team of gunmen had looked at a couple of possible buildings, but Franco, as the senior marksman, had ruled them out as the motorcade would not be in sight long enough for multiple shots to be taken.

'What about that building over there?' asked Paolo. 'It looks ideal from here.'

'Yes, you could be right,' mused Gabrielli. 'It's right on the corner of Elm Street and Houston Street, and the motorcade will have to slow right down here for this sharp left turn. Let's find out what the building is.' They all walked over to the building to discover it was actually the Texas School Book Depository, a seven-floor building facing Dealey Plaza in Dallas. Located at 411 Elm Street on the northwest corner of Elm and North Houston Streets, it was absolutely perfect. It overlooked two streets on the route, and it had numerous windows. Gabrielli walked into the entrance with Franco, leaving the others waiting outside. He asked the receptionist if he could have a look around as he was looking for some new commercial premises to rent in the area. He was given permission to look round, but warned that the top two floors were incredibly untidy due to some ongoing reconstruction work. The young receptionist said a lady would happily show them round. Gabrielli did his best to talk her out of accompanying them, but she insisted.

The building was currently in use as a multi-floor warehouse for the storage of thousands of school textbooks and other related materials, and as an order-fulfilment center by the Texas School Book Depository Company, a privately-owned corporation. According to the highly officious lady who showed them round, sometime after the company moved in, it was found that the upper floors had sustained quite bad oil damage from items stored there by the previous tenant, a wholesaler grocer. So, in order to protect the company's books, which were all stored in cardboard boxes, from oil seeping up from the floor, a process had begun to cover the top two floors with plywood. Work had begun on the west side of both the sixth and seventh floors, leaving both floors in total chaos with stock shifted as far as the east wall, and stacks in between piled unusually high. Franco and Gabrielli were now on the top floor, the seventh, and from here they could see everything. Franco wandered over to the window and looked down Elm Street. Gabrielli left the officious and now quite annoying woman who had been showing them around, saying he needed to consult with his colleague. He walked over and joined Franco at the window.

'This place is perfect,' said Franco as quietly as he could so as not to be heard by the annoying woman who wouldn't leave them in peace. 'I've got a clear view of virtually the entire length of Elm Street. If I wait until they've passed me, I can then shoot them from behind. Nobody is ever watching behind themselves, and nor will the President's security people.'

'What about Oswald,' asked Gabrielli.

'Simple, boss. I'll shoot from up here on the seventh floor, and he can do exactly the same thing one floor lower on the sixth. Even if the car speeds up and heads off down Elm Street, once they realize they're being shot at, they'll be driving straight towards the other two guns.'

'OK, that sounds good, but we still need to find two more decent locations,' said Gabrielli.

'Look down there to your right, boss,' said Franco quite quietly, again making sure they were not heard by their escort. 'A couple of hundred yards down the road. If you continue down Elm Street, that is, the way the motorcade will be travelling, there's a small hill, a sort of grassy knoll with a fence on it. One of the other guns could be behind that picket fence for cover. He'd get a really great shot with the car heading towards him, and I'm sure a couple of our guys dressed in police uniforms could easily keep any nosey spectators away from the area.'

'Sounds good to me, Franco,' said Gabrielli. 'Let's go and have a closer look.'

Jacques was just entering his fourth different laundry/dry cleaners of the day. He'd had no luck so far, but it didn't bother him; he'd just keep going until he found the one he wanted. Entering the premises, he faced a young lady behind the counter.

'Good day, and how may we help you today, sir?' she asked, but even before she'd said a word he knew immediately he'd found exactly the place he needed. Hanging on the rack behind the counter, waiting for collection, were at least a dozen Dallas Police Uniforms. He'd seen what he wanted, so he simply turned around and left the premises without uttering a single word.

'Huh, some people can be incredibly rude without even opening their mouths,' muttered the girl behind the counter.

Giuseppe had also located exactly what he wanted. He'd been studying a map of this part of Texas, telephone directories and chatting to locals, and as a result, he'd found a nice little military base and service store, just outside Dallas, at a place called Rowlett, near Lake Ray Hubbard. He could hardly just walk in and ask to borrow a few two-way radio sets, so it unfortunately meant breaking in, probably in the middle of the night. He thought long and hard about it, and eventually decided there would be just four of them needed; two inside and two outside keeping watch. He'd clear it with Gabrielli at the update meeting that same evening. Rafael had been on his own all day, touring round gun shops, and looking for those establishments that specialized in hunting rifles. Rafael had spoken to Franco, Bernardo and Paolo, and all three said they wanted exactly the same rifle; the Remington Model 700. Introduced in 1962 as a sleeker and much better turned-out version of the Company's Model 721, 722, and 725 sporting rifles, the three gunmen all agreed it was the best rifle for the job. The Remington Model 700 is a bolt-action hunting rifle with an attractive and functionally shaped walnut stock, with an action loosely based on the Mauser 98 concept, but modified to allow cheaper manufacturing costs. However, it also incorporated several new and key improvements, including near Wetherby-like strength, with three rings of steel surrounding the cartridge head, a very fast lock time, a natural and easy to use two-position safety and an excellent trigger mechanism. The push feed action uses a plunger ejector and a circlip extractor, both mounted in a recessed bolt face. The open top receiver is round because it is simply drilled from steel bar stock. The recoil lug is essentially a heavy-duty steel washer trapped between the barrel and the receiver. Cartridges are fed from an internal, staggered box magazine formed from sheet steel. The trigger guard/bottom iron is made from aluminum. Without doubt, all three men agreed, what they needed were three Remington Model 700's with telescopic sights.

In total, Rafael visited eleven different gun stores that day. Four couldn't help him at all, but he eventually managed to buy the three rifles he needed in three different stores; two of them located in Dallas itself and one from a store in Fort Worth. He bought the three specific telescopic sights he'd been instructed to acquire in three other stores, all in Dallas, and 250 rounds of ammunition in a seventh store, this one located just outside Fort Worth. He'd used most of Gabrielli's cash, but at least he'd completed his task in a day. He'd done well, he thought to himself, as he drove back to the White Plaza with his seven purchases all locked safely away in the boot of the car. Gabrielli, Franco, Bernardo and Paolo had all reached the fence on the grassy knoll, and were looking back up Elm Street towards the Texas Book Depository. The fence was about five feet high and was made of plain wooden planks, all nailed to wooden crossbeams. The top of each plank had been made into a point, and therefore any two next to each other made a perfect V-shape; the ideal resting place for supporting the business end of a high-powered rifle.

'This is the perfect spot for the second gunman,' said Paolo 'The President will just drive towards me making the target area bigger and bigger the nearer he gets. I can hide behind the fence, and with a couple of our guys standing in front of it, they can keep people away until we're ready to shoot. Also, if you don't mind me suggesting it, boss, if we were all in police uniforms, nobody will bother us anyway.'

'Good point, Paolo,' replied Gabrielli, 'and, of course, I don't mind. Anything that helps the mission. I'll tell Jacques we're going to need more uniforms. Any ideas about the third location, Bernardo?'

'Well, I've got two possibilities in mind. One is very well hidden, but probably incredibly smelly, and the other is much easier, but fairly public.'

'Tell me about the smelly one,' laughed Gabrielli.

'I was thinking of inside that manhole or drain cover thing over there,' he said, pointing. 'The President's car will have to drive within twenty feet of the position and I couldn't miss, but I'm pretty sure it will stink to high heaven, and the smell might even make me pass out'

'What about your other location?' asked Gabrielli.

'I was thinking about over there, on the flyover,' he answered, pointing.

'Actually, I think that's a railway overpass, or railway bridge,' said Franco. 'I saw a train going over it about five minutes ago.'

'I think that'll do nicely, guys,' said Gabrielli. 'It's the perfect spot for the third gun. Again, it's higher, giving you good sight lines, and you will be looking down, and secondly, there are some reasonably thick concrete pillars up there to take cover behind, and as in the previous location, the motorcade will have to drive towards you, giving you plenty of time to line up your shot.'

'So, are we happy with those three locations then, boss?' asked Paolo.

'Oh yes,' replied Gabrielli. 'I think we're in business, gentlemen.'

Chapter Forty-Four
September 1963
The White House, Washington D.C.

'Good morning, Jack,' said Bobby as he entered the Oval Office. The President was quietly working through some papers at his desk. He put his pen down, took a couple of mouthfuls of coffee, then, moving out from behind the desk, he beckoned Bobby to join him on the sofas.

'Bobby,' he said quietly. 'What the hell's happened to Sally? I still haven't heard from her for months; she seems to have just disappeared off the face of the planet.'

'Your guess is as good as mine, Jack,' replied Bobby. 'I got one of our guys to make enquiries at the night club, but they still haven't seen her either. I hate to repeat myself, Jack, but I honestly think the Vatican has had her done away with. I know you don't agree, but I'm afraid that's my honest opinion. If you don't mind me asking, Jack, who are you seeing these days? Sally, as you say, has completely disappeared, Marilyn's sadly died, and we both think that was pretty suspicious, and it could be the Vatican again. If they'll kill one, they'll kill two even easier. I know Mary Meyer said she couldn't see you anymore, and we're both pretty sure she was scared and had been warned off. Pam Turnure decided to leave Jackie's employ and get work elsewhere. Who's left?'

'Well as you know from the "committee meetings", I'm still seeing Mimi Alford occasionally, and then, of course, there's Priscilla and Jill.'

'Oh come on bro, be careful with those two, Jack. You do know that around the White House, Priscilla Wear and Jill Cowen are known by your security detail as Fiddle and

Faddle. The problem is, Jack, the two women are known more for their closeness to you rather than for their level of hard work as White House employees. Neither of them ever does much work and according to reports I've received, they both leave work frequently to go skinny-dipping in the pool with you. They then go back to their stations with wet hair, somewhat giving the game away. You need to be a lot more careful with all these women, Jack. I mean, if you don't mind me saying, it was pretty dumb taking them both on international trips like you did to Berlin. Sorry, Jack, but that was just plain stupid. Plus, you also took them to Rome, Ireland, Costa Rica, Mexico and Nassau. Jackie is not stupid, and I have to tell you without any doubt, she is not in the dark any longer about any of this, Jack.'

'You mean she knows about them both?'

'Yes, Jack, she knows about them both, and she knew about Sally, and Marilyn, and Mary, and all the others. She still loves you, Jack, and she's decided to live with it, but that doesn't mean she has to like it. Come on, Jack, it's just not fair on the mother of your kids.'

'So what am I supposed to do, Bobby? You know how I feel about women. They are my passion, my hobby.'

'If I wasn't your younger brother, Jack, I'd tell you to grow up, take responsibility for your life and in particular, act like a husband and a father to your family. Find yourself a new, less hurtful hobby, Jack. But you are my older brother, so I won't say any of that!'

'I think you just did, but I know you mean well so never mind. Tell me then, Bobby, what the hell do I do about Mimi?' asked the President.

'How long have you been seeing her now, Jack?'

'Well, I suppose it started back in the summer of 1962. A few days after she started her internship in the White House press office, she met me while taking a midday dip in the White House pool. I swam up and introduced myself and later that day sent word that she was invited to after-work drinks. I offered to give her a private tour of the house, which culminated in sleeping with her. Apparently, she was only 19 at the time, and I was her first.'

'Well, that has to stop as well, Jack. Kick her into touch. Your wife can only take so much, and if you don't knock all this on the head soon, I think Jackie will walk out on you, and take the kids with her. If she does leave you, Jack, I promise you you'll never get over it, and you'll certainly never get re-elected.'

'Let me think about it, Bobby.'

'Look, Jack, I know this is a difficult time for both you and Jackie having just lost your son. What was it the doctor called it?'

'Hyaline membrane decease.'

'Yeah, that was it,' said Bobby.

'God Bobby, Patrick; that's what we were naming him, was only two days old. I know he was five and half weeks premature, but his death was still unexpected and it still hurts like mad. But I've still got to carry on.'

'I know, Jack, but try concentrating on work. Tell me, what you thought of this Martin Luther King character,' asked Bobby.

'That man is incredible. His "I have a dream" speech will, I'm sure, go down in history as one of the most important speeches of the twentieth century. I chatted privately with him here at the White House, and I tell you, that man will go far.'

'If he lives long enough,' commented Bobby.

'What do you mean?' asked the President.

'You and I both loved his speech, as did millions of others, but there are also thousands of people out there who hate everything he stands for, and it only needs one with a gun.'

'God, Bobby, you're scaring me now. America's not that bad, is it?'

'Come on, Jack, you're the President, and you know damn well it is that bad. There are a lot of people out there who think the answer to everything they don't like is to simply point a gun at whatever or whoever they don't like, and pull the trigger. We make life so easy in this country for people to buy guns, and then all it needs for some nutcase to decide to take the law into his own hands. I tell you, Jack, it's a bloody miracle nobody has taken a pot shot at the pair of us yet.'

'Give them time, Bobby,' laughed Jack 'give them time.'

Chapter Forty-Five
October 1963
The Vatican, Rome, Italy

Giovanni Battista Montini, now known to the world as Pope Paul VI, was seated in his private quarters when the Camerlengo, Cardinal Benedetto Aloisi Masella, knocked on his door, but waited instead of just walking in as was his custom with the previous incumbent. He simply waited outside for permission to enter. The Camerlengo's relationship with the new Pope was fine and they got on very well, but it was not the same close relationship as the personal friendship he'd had with the previous Pope. The Pope called him in and invited him to sit down.

'I notice, Camerlengo,' he began as the Camerlengo entered, 'that several of my staff from the Holy Office appear to be away on what has been listed simply as business. Do you have any idea what the nature of this business is, and where it has taken them?'

Cardinal Masella thought quickly to himself. His reasoning was simple: If I tell the Pope everything I know he will undoubtedly start asking lots of difficult questions which could easily backfire on me, and it could also harm the memory and the legacy of Pope John XXIII. So, on due consideration, the Camerlengo decided that playing ignorant was by far the best policy. After all, the only other person that knew all the details was now sadly deceased, so Pope John XXIII would not be telling anyone what he'd started, and there was nothing in writing. This all went through his mind in about five seconds, and he used the thinking time to pull over a chair and sit down.

'I'm afraid I have no idea, Holy Father,' he at last replied. 'All I know is that they were all working on something considered extremely important, at the specific request of, and on the personal commission of your predecessor, Pope John XXIII. But I'm afraid he did not inform me of either the nature of the task, or of its location.'

'I see,' mused the Pope. 'Have you any idea when we may see Signor Gabrielli and his colleagues returning to Rome, and perhaps starting to work for the current Pope, rather than the previous occupant of this post?'

'As I said, Holy Father,' began Masella, 'I have no idea when they'll be back.'

At least he was telling the truth with that last statement.

Chapter Forty-Six
Early November 1963
Dallas, Texas

Things were falling nicely into place, Gabrielli told himself. Jacques had taken Mario, Theodore and Salvador with him, and the four of them had headed for the laundry and dry cleaners Jacques had found the previous month. They'd gone there the same night as the day he'd found it as they wanted to grab the uniforms he'd seen. They arrived at the front of the shop about two o'clock in the morning, and then walked to the end of the block, up the side road and then down a rear alley that took them to the back of the shop. Theodore (or Theo as he was called by everyone) went to the far end of the alley to keep watch, while Salvador (or Sal) stayed at the end of the alley they'd just entered. Jacques and Mario, checking that all was clear in both directions, walked down the alley until they reached the rear entrance of the laundry. The door was pretty solid, but there was a window next to it, the bottom sill of which was about five feet off the ground. Jacques stood on Mario's shoulders, and he started to work the window with a knife and a crowbar. After about three minutes, he'd done enough damage to the area where the upper and lower sashes met, and then slid his knife in the gap and used it to push the slide bar open that held the two windows together. He slid the bottom window up, and then dropped quietly inside the shop. Having found a chair, he stood on it, leaned out of the window and helped Mario inside. They started searching the racks of dry-cleaned clothes, and found a total of eleven pairs of police trousers, and two smart officer's jackets. On the laundry racks, they found ten police shirts, all complete with embroidered badges and rank epaulettes where appropriate. Unfortunately, they found no caps, belts or any of the other bits and pieces police officers wore with their shirts and trousers. Still, what they had gotten was a good start, but Jacques realized they would have to try a few theatrical costumiers in the morning, preferably before the cleaners reported the uniforms had been stolen. So, the following morning, Jacques, Marco, Mario, Sal and Theo were all waiting for the doors of five different theatrical costumiers to open. Two in Dallas, two in Fort Worth, and one in Arlington. They hired absolutely everything they could get their hands on that was police related. Caps, belts, holsters, truncheons, whistles etc., etc. By the time they got it all back to the hotel, they had enough equipment to make up eight complete police uniforms. More than enough for what they needed.

Gabrielli was keen to get his hands on the radio sets they needed, so they planned to break in to the little military base and service store in Rowlett that same night. They set off at 1.00 am and parked the car about half a mile away around 1.45 am. There were six of them squashed into the bigger of the two cars they'd got, a large Pontiac sedan. Gabrielli who was in charge, Giuseppe who had to be there as he was the only one who would recognize what they were looking for, Mario, Theo and Sal who could provide muscle if needed, and Franco who would happily shoot anyone trying to interfere with them (but in such a way as to not kill him). Gabrielli really didn't want the United States Army hunting them down for killing one of their own; a soldier. They were all dressed from head-to-toe in black. Black running shoes for comfort and silence, black socks, black trousers and black roll neck sweaters. Gabrielli had also bought along six of the ten black woolen balaclavas from a ski shop he'd found in Washington D.C. before they'd gone to Dallas. Gabrielli had always been good at forward planning.

Upon their arrival, they walked quietly along the boundary fence until they reached the wire fence surrounding the base. Mario cut through the wire and held it open while the other five crawled through, then Sal held it open while

Mario crawled through. They then pulled the wired back into place, and then Sal held it together again with three pieces of dark green string. The stores were located in quite a large red brick building on the far side of the base, which was fortunately well away from the main road and the barracks block. They slowly worked their way round the fence until they had reached the far side. They took cover behind a couple of large oil tanks and watched for guards for five minutes. There appeared to be none walking the grounds, so they ran quietly to the side of the building where they all stopped to catch their breath. Gabrielli and Franco weren't as young as the rest of them, and they needed a few extra minutes to get their breath back. Giuseppe had, meanwhile, found a window and tried it. It was locked, but he could see it was only a simple catch which would easily open with a knife, but he didn't know who or what would be waiting on the inside. Theo joined him under the window, and bent down on all fours so that Giuseppe could stand on his back and look inside the store. As far as he could see, it was all clear. Gabrielli gave him the go ahead, and he slid his knife into the gap, pushed the catch aside and pulled open the window. They all climbed inside and pulled the window closed behind them.

'Nobody can switch on their torches or any lights,' commanded Gabrielli in a whisper. 'Just let your eyes get acclimatized to the darkness, and you'll soon be able to see well.' They all did as he'd suggested, and indeed, their eyesight improved greatly. 'Mario, you and Theo go and check there's nobody about. If you have to, use the chloroform you brought on anyone you find, but no killing. OK?'

'Yes boss,' replied Mario, and he and Theo did a tour of the inside of the stores. 'All clear,' said Mario when he got back.

'OK,' began Gabrielli. 'You all know what we're looking for, and remember, no lights, and only speak if you have to, and for God's sake, keep to whispers.'

They all separated into different directions, and started searching the shelves. There must have been over two hundred shelves of different widths, and all set at different heights as this was quite a large store. Although the base itself was quite small personnel-wise, it was responsible for supplying the needs of most of the military bases located in Texas with whatever they needed. After fifteen minutes of searching, they had found nothing, and then Sal whispered, 'I think I've found some radios.'

Giuseppe and Gabrielli quickly went over and joined him. Sure enough, he'd found the section of the stores stocking radios. The first ones he looked at were no use for what they needed them for, but on the shelf above, Giuseppe found two large wooden crates, one of which contained exactly what they needed; ten HT-1E walkie-talkie sets.

'Just take the entire crate,' instructed Gabrielli. Giuseppe and Sal carefully took down the wooden crate, and then, carrying it by the rope handles located at each end, they carefully carried it over to the window. Mario was about to push the window open when he heard talking outside. Gabrielli motioned everyone to get down onto the floor and keep quiet while he took a peek out of the window. There were two soldiers standing chatting just outside the stores having a quiet smoke, about twenty feet to his left.

'I can easily shoot them, boss,' whispered Franco.

'No, Franco,' replied Gabrielli, 'show a little patience. We'll just wait until they've finished their cigarettes and moved on.'

In fact, it took the two soldiers over ten minutes, and then they stamped out their cigarette stubs, picked them up and dumped them in a red fire bucket, turned away and then headed towards the barracks block, still chatting. Looking both to his left and right, as far as he was able to see; nobody was in sight. Gabrielli gently pushed the window open and looked again in both directions. Everything was clear, so, using sign language only, he indicated to everyone to climb out, which they did, with Mario bringing up the rear and closing the window. Mario then inserted his knife back in the gap, and after several failed attempts, he eventually managed to push the slide catch across, relocking the window. They all then worked their way round the inside of the perimeter fence until they reached the cut in the wire. Sal untied the three pieces of string and the six men and their crate of radios crawled through the gap. Sal tied it back up again, and they all headed back to the Pontiac. An hour later, they were all back at the hotel, radios now sorted, and catching some well-earned sleep.

Chapter Forty-Seven
Mid November 1963
The Vatican, Rome, Italy

Pope Paul VI picked up the telephone on his desk and asked to be put through directly to the desk of Signor Antonio Cavalli. In Gabrielli's absence, and as Deputy Head of the Holy Office, Cavalli was temporarily running the Holy Office. He had picked up the telephone, not having been warned who was calling him.

'Yes,' he yelled down the phone, 'what the hell is it? I'm incredibly busy and I haven't got time to waste, so this better be important.'

'Well, I think it's important, Signor Cavalli,' replied the Pope, 'and I would appreciate a minute or two of your obviously very busy time.'

'And who the hell might you be?' demanded Cavalli.

'Well Signor, when I looked in the mirror this morning,' began the Holy Father, 'I was Pope Paul VI, and as far as I am aware, that is still the case.'

Cavalli jumped out of his skin and shot to his feet, even though nobody could see him. 'Holy Father,' he stuttered. 'I am so sorry, I had no idea it was you, and I must apologize profusely, but with Signor Gabrielli having been away for so long, I am rushed off my feet and I am afraid my usually calm temperament is being somewhat strained at the moment.'

'I understand completely, Signor, so do not worry. However, I would be very grateful if you could please try to find some time in that incredibly busy schedule of yours to visit me in my private office, at your earliest convenience, of course.'

'I will leave this instant, Holy Father. I should be with you in ten minutes.'

'Thank you,' said the Pope, putting the telephone back on its cradle and smiling to himself. He'd decided he needed to know exactly where Gabrielli was, and what on earth he was doing. After all, Gabrielli worked for him now, not the deceased Pope John XXIII. He had tried asking the Camerlengo, but Cardinal Masella claimed he had no idea where he was or what he was doing. He really shouldn't doubt the word of his Camerlengo, but he knew how close the two men had been, and he couldn't believe the Camerlengo knew nothing. At least Signor Cavalli should know, but if he didn't, then how on earth was he to find out? These were the thoughts going through his mind as Antonio Cavalli made his way to the Pope's private office in the Vatican.

There was a knock on his door, and Antonio Cavalli was ushered into the Pope's private office by one of the many priests who looked after the Holy Father's needs. Cavalli entered, lowered his head and kissed the Pope's extended hand as was the custom. Antonio Cavalli was not at all like Gabrielli, his boss. Gabrielli was only five-foot six inches tall, and quite stocky, whereas Cavalli was quite tall, being nearly six-foot two inches in fact, and he was fairly thin in build. Unlike the "interesting" face of the confirmed single man Claudio Gabrielli, Cavalli was quite good-looking as his wife Francesca was always quick to tell everyone.

Cavalli had been born and brought up in Florence, and he had spent most of his working life in the Cabilierri; the Italian Police. He was initially in uniform for two years, and then he was offered the chance of becoming a detective. He jumped at the opportunity and started by investigating jewelry thefts from several shops that were all located on the world-famous Ponte Vecchio. For anyone who does not know Florence, the Ponte Vecchio is the wonderful medieval bridge that straddles the Arno River running through the center of Florence. The unusual thing about the bridge is that it is entirely covered with jewelry shops, on both sides of the road running across the entire span, and from one end to the other. In medieval times, they all started out as butchers' shops, but over time, things changed, people changed and Florence changed. By the time Cavalli started his career in the Cabilierri, they were all high-end jewelry shops, with two-story houses on top of them.

There had been a series of robberies in these shops on the Ponte Vecchio, and Cavalli's boss, who was feeling very overworked and needed this like he needed a hole in the head, was keen to get rid of it. So he decided to assign the case to young Cavalli. It was his very first investigation, and even he would later admit that he'd been incredibly fortunate. His young cousin Angelo had become a very minor thief in the city, mixing with all the wrong types, and after his older cousin had applied some family pressure, his cousin tipped him off about who the thieves were, but only on condition his name was never mentioned. Antonio Cavalli was young, keen to get on, and more than happy to take all the credit. He cleared the whole thing up in less than a week, not only apprehending all the thieves, but also managing, in the process, to return all the stolen property to its rightful owners. The shopkeepers of Florence all thought he was a true genius, and the citizens of Florence all loved their bright new investigative officer. As a direct result of his lightning success, he had become a minor celebrity in Florence, even getting his photograph in the local newspapers. Due to his good fortune and, in fairness, his hard work, he quickly rose to the rank of Inspector. Then, two years ago, at the age of thirty-seven he had gotten married. His new wife, Francesca, who was scared every day that her new husband was about to be shot to death, month after month encouraged him to leave the police, and to start looking for something just a little bit safer. After roughly eighteen months of constant requests, he finally acquiesced and started looking for a new job.

He'd heard about the Vatican vacancy one lunchtime while chatting with a Holy Office staffer over a glass of wine and a pasta meal in a local bar. He decided to get some more details from the personnel people at the Holy Office regarding what would be required of a Deputy Head, salary levels, working hours, etc. With all the facts and figures at his disposal, he sat down one evening and spent over two hours discussing it thoroughly with his wife. They agreed he should apply, and after a lengthy interview with a panel of five Cardinals, including the Camerlengo, he was offered the job, which he gratefully accepted. Signor Claudio Gabrielli, who would be his direct boss, had not even been consulted, just informed of Signor Antonio Cavalli's appointment, but that was how the Roman Catholic Church did things. Francesca was thrilled about the new job as it meant more money for working less hours, but most importantly, her husband was unlikely to be killed working for the Roman Catholic Church. After all, they didn't get involved with death and murder, did they?

'So, Signor Cavalli,' began the Pope, 'can you please tell me where Signor Gabrielli is, and what is he doing that is so important, that it has kept him away from his duties here at the Vatican for months on end?'

'I wish I knew, Holy Father,' answered Cavalli, 'but the Holy Office has no information on file regarding Signor Gabrielli's whereabouts, and nobody seems to have any idea where he is or what he is up to. All we do know for sure is that whatever the task is, it was given to him personally by Pope John XXIII. What I can tell you, however, is that he has taken Signor Mario Orsini from the Holy Office with him, and it is believed that they are both somewhere in the United States of America. It is also believed that Signor Gabrielli has also taken several other men to assist him that do not work for the Holy Office. This is only "office gossip" you understand, Holy Father, and I cannot confirm any of the information I have just given you.'

'I see,' mused the Pope. 'Tell me, does Signor Gabrielli ever telephone the Holy Office to report in, or to find out what is happening back here in the Vatican?'

'No, not that I am aware of, Holy Father, not since he left.'

Pope Paul VI made his decision.

'As of this moment, Signor Claudio Gabrielli is suspended from his role within the Holy Office, and I am appointing you, Signor Cavalli, to take over as the new head. You will report only to me, and your first task is to try and locate Signor Gabrielli, and then inform him that his presence is required back here at the Vatican immediately. Signor Orsini is likewise suspended, and neither of them is to do or say anything in the name of the Vatican. Find them, get them to stop whatever it is they are doing, Signor, and bring them back here to speak to me. Do I make myself clear?'

'Perfectly, Holy Father. I will get on to it straightaway. Two questions though, if I may ask.'

'Yes?' asked the Pope.

'If necessary, do I have your permission to travel to the United States and try to force them to return to Italy and the Vatican? And if I do find them, should I inform Signor Gabrielli of his suspension?'

'You most certainly have my permission to travel to America should it prove necessary, but I would like to reserve the pleasure of telling Signor Gabrielli of my decision myself, unless, of course, you find you need to tell him yourself in order to assert your authority.'

'Understood, Holy Father, and thank you for your faith in me.'

'You will, of course,' continued the Pope, 'receive the greatly increased salary that goes with your new position, plus the sole use of the Holy Office limousine and chauffeur that was previously reserved for the use of Signor Gabrielli. All I ask of you is that you don't let me down.'

'Thank you, Holy Father, and I will, of course, do all that is humanly possible.'

'Thankfully, my son, we are not limited to only what is humanly possible, and in this line of work, we can all call on a much greater source of help if required. Please keep me informed of your progress, and I look forward to your undoubted success.'

Antonio Cavalli, the new head of the Holy Office, left the Vatican and walked slowly back to his office deep in thought, wondering how on earth he was supposed to find Claudio Gabrielli, a man who, it would appear, really didn't want to be found.

Chapter Forty-Eight
Mid-November 1963
Dallas, Texas

Gabrielli, of course, knew nothing of what had just taken place at the Vatican. He wasn't in the least bit interested in finding out anything about life back in Rome until he had completed his task in the United States. It was, without a shadow of doubt to his mind, a Holy task, given to him by the Holy Father. As it had been a direct commission from the Holy Father, he would not let him down. Of course, it would have been far easier if President Kennedy had been a reasonable man and a decent, honorable Catholic who had listened to the Holy Father's instructions, clearly explained to him by Bishop O'Boyle, taken heed and changed his ways. But he had not been. Nor too were several of the women he had spoken to. Some he had managed to frighten off, but sadly not all. There had been that dreadful Sally Gilchrist woman, the stroppy blonde stripper who just would not listen, and who, simply because of her own stubbornness, was now buried in the Texas desert. Then there was poor Marilyn Monroe, the world-famous film actress with the world and untold riches at her feet. But would she listen? No. She too had thought she could do whatever she wanted because of her fame. Well, she'd sadly learnt otherwise, and Gabrielli had taken no pleasure in her death. Nevertheless, he had been particularly gratified when the papers and later, the coroner reported that she had died from a self-inflicted accidental overdose. As far as he could tell, nothing they had done could be laid at his door, or more importantly, at the door of the Vatican.

Now, he was just days away from completing the task Pope John XXIII had set him all those months ago. He wished he could have confirmed the instructions and his plan with the Holy Father, and be a hundred percent sure that he was definitely happy for stage three to go ahead, but sadly, the Pope had died, and he could hardly ask the new one. He'd never met Pope Paul VI, as he'd been busy in America when the man he was working for, very sadly, went to meet his beloved maker. But the last thing Pope John had said to him during their last conversation was, 'Don't let this American President bring shame on the Holy Catholic Church.' What they were about to do was, in Gabrielli's mind, the only way of fulfilling Pope John's wishes, and so stage three it had to be.

Gabrielli got in the car and drove to the Texas Book Depository where Lee Harvey Oswald had managed to obtain a temporary position that gave him access to the sixth floor. He met him over lunch, and talked through how much the CIA were relying on him. Gabrielli had previously shown Oswald fake IDs that purported to be from the CIA, and he confirmed that Oswald was going to shoot the President in conjunction with other CIA operatives, in order that JFK could not continue to take America down the path of destruction he was leading them on.

Gabrielli had found Lee Harvey Oswald several months earlier by frequently visiting various communist clubs, going to hear prominent communist speakers at rallies and seeing who turned up to listen. Oswald regularly turned up to meetings and rallies, and Gabrielli decided he was worth approaching. Initially, they sat and chatted in general over a cup of coffee, and Gabrielli soon realized Oswald could be easily played and set up as the patsy if and when the time came. It had still been "if" at that stage, but the time for action might well come, and Gabrielli liked to have everything and everyone in place, just in case. He started running down JFK to Oswald, and found he was extremely easy to manipulate. When he first mentioned the vague idea of assassination by someone, Oswald was quick to agree that, in his opinion, it would undoubtedly be in America's best interest if Kennedy was dead. So Gabrielli then tentatively broached the idea of the CIA putting a team of covert gunmen together, and being an ex-military man himself, would Oswald be interested in becoming one of the team. He laid it on really thick, pandering to Oswald's ego, and pretty soon, Lee Harvey Oswald had signed up to do his bit for the future of the United States of America, thinking he was working with the CIA. Gabrielli had taken his time, but over the course of three months, he had persuaded Lee Harvey Oswald to assassinate JFK.

Chapter Forty-Nine
November 19th, 1963
The Palace of the Holy Office
Rome, Italy

Antonio Cavalli was a very happy man, and his wife, Francesca, was even happier. In fact, it would be fair to say she was totally ecstatic. She had been brought up in a relatively poor family, her father being a carpenter, and her mother simply running the home and looking after Francesca and her two older sisters. She had been brought up a devout Catholic from birth, and now, here she was, married to the handsome man she desperately loved, having just discovered from her doctor that she was not losing her figure because she was getting fat, but because she was pregnant with their first child. Her husband was now not only working for the Vatican, he had been appointed by the Pope himself to run the Holy Office. His work address was now a palace, he was without doubt at the top of his profession, and to cap it all, he had a chauffeur-driven limousine at his disposal twenty-four hours a day. Life just couldn't get better.

Antonio Cavalli was also happy, but not quite as happy as his wife. Yes, he'd gotten the top job, the limo, the chauffeur, and they could now afford virtually anything they wanted, but despite all of this, he had a massive problem. He had no idea where to start in his search for Gabrielli. He might have the job for the moment, but if he didn't find his ex-boss and bring him back soon, he thought the job would disappear, and so would his career. He'd done very little other than think over the last couple of days, and all he'd come up with was one idea. Somebody, somewhere must know where Gabrielli was. And then he realized he thought he now knew who that somebody was.

Cardinal Benedetto Aloisi Masella – The Camerlengo

Cavalli left the Palace and made his way over to the Vatican. One great advantage of this new job was that he didn't have to report to anyone other than the Pope himself. He went anywhere he wanted, whenever he wanted, and nobody, not even the world-famous Swiss Guard tried to stop him. He arrived at the Camerlengo's office and thought about just barging in, but no, he was still a gentleman at heart, and he would show the Camerlengo the due respect he deserved. He knocked on the door and after receiving a polite "come in", he did just that.

'Ah, Signor Cavalli, my congratulations on your promotion and your new role at the Palace of the Holy Office.'

'Thank you, Camerlengo, and it is in connection with that new role that I have come to see you.'

'Please sit down, my friend, and tell me how I can help you.'

'You can help me, Cardinal, by being very honest with me, and by telling me everything you know about Signor Gabrielli, where exactly he is in the United States, and what the task it is that he is still undertaking on behalf of Pope John XXIII. I must apologize for speaking to you in this somewhat rude manner, but before you tell me you know nothing, may I just say that I have been specifically asked by the Holy Father, who needless to say, we all now serve, to find Signor Gabrielli and bring him back to the Vatican. Please, Camerlengo, I beg of you. Whatever the commission was that Gabrielli undertook, surely it died when Pope John did?'

'You speak extremely wisely for one so young, Signor Cavalli' replied the Camerlengo. 'You are right in pointing out, in your gentle reminder, that I have indeed been very remiss in my duties and obligations to our new Pope, but I assure you it has been simply out of love and respect for the wishes of our previous Holy Father, who also happened to be my best friend in this lonely world that is the Vatican. Sadly, I cannot tell you exactly where to find Signor Gabrielli at this moment in time, because I simply do not know. However, what I can tell you, and perhaps what I should have shared with someone ages ago, is what exactly he was asked to do by Pope John XXIII, who I assure you, only had the best interests of the Catholic Church at heart. The commission was in essence very simple, but I fear it became more complicated as time passed, and if I'm honest, I fear that with the sad death of Pope John, Signor Gabrielli, in his desire to fulfil the late Pope's wishes, has probably now taken matters into his own hands.'

The Camerlengo started at the beginning, and told Cavalli everything he knew about Claudio Gabrielli's two-stage plan, or at least; the version he'd been told about. He then told Cavalli that he knew there was a stage three, and what he surmised it involved, even though he didn't know for sure, despite Pope John having given him a very vague idea. Nearly two hours after he had arrived at the Camerlengo's office, Cavalli walked slowly back to his own office deep in thought and started to make his own plans.

The first stage of his own plan was simple. Use his own brain and try to get inside the mind of Gabrielli now that he knew more or less what he was up to. He had gotten to know him reasonably well, he thought, having worked together for several months before he did his disappearing trick, and now that he knew the nature of the task in America, he understood why he, an ex-police inspector, hadn't been included in Gabrielli's plans. The first thing Gabrielli would do, he felt sure, would be to get his hands on the President's schedule in order to find out where he was going to be at any given time. So, he reasoned, he needed to do the same. Cavalli thought long and hard about his options, and although he didn't want to, he realized that he only really had the one option open to him if he was to make any progress. So, very reluctantly, he contacted an old girlfriend who he knew now worked in the U.S. Embassy in Rome, and after a lot of apologizing for how he had broken up with her six years earlier, he eventually persuaded her to let him have a copy of JFK's appointments for the next two months. That, he felt sure, would be long enough to find Signor Gabrielli.

He walked round to the U.S. Embassy and collected the sealed plain brown envelope she had left for him with the front receptionist. He did not open it until he was safely back behind his own desk with the door closed at the Palace of the Holy Office. Ninety minutes later, he boarded a plane headed for Dallas.

Chapter Fifty
November 20th, 1963
Dallas, Texas

Gabrielli called them all together in his hotel suite to talk through the requirements for the day, and to have a full-dress parade.

'Why the hell do we have to dress up like this, boss?' protested Franco.

'You said it yourself,' replied Gabrielli. 'Because I'm the boss and I say so. Look, three days from now we're going to be walking the streets of Dallas dressed as cops. We might not know or notice if part of the uniform doesn't look right, but real cops sure will. We can't afford to get anything wrong, so all of you – get changed and quit the damn moaning.'

Ten minutes later, they were all being inspected by Jacques, who had been charged by Gabrielli a few days earlier with finding out and noting every scrap of information he could about Dallas police uniforms. He'd chatted to cops off-duty in cafes and sat outside a bar watching various cops come and go from the police station on the opposite side of the road. He'd taken a few discreet photographs of uniformed officers, and he'd even drawn pictures to help him make sure he got every aspect correct.

'You're wearing the handgun on the wrong side, Theo,' he said.

'I know,' he replied, 'but I'm left-handed.'

'That doesn't matter,' countered Gabrielli. 'It just looks wrong and someone might pick you up on it. Besides,' he continued laughing, 'it's not as if you're going to need to pull out the revolver quick-draw style when you decide to do your civic duty and arrest someone, is it?' They all laughed, and Theo moved the handgun to his other hip. They all then went through the same rigorous inspection parade, and Gabrielli realized what an excellent job Jacques had done. He told him so as he thanked him for the care he'd put into the task he'd been given. Gabrielli always found people reacted much better to carrots than sticks.

'OK, all of you. Get back into your everyday clothes and we'll meet in the hotel lobby in ten minutes. We're going to walk the route and make sure nothing has changed in the last twenty-four hours. We can't be too careful, and we'll only get one chance at this, so everyone, keep your wits about you and keep your eyes open.'

Once they were all changed, they walked the short distance to the Texas Book Depository, and from there, they slowly walked the route JFK's limousine would be driving. Giuseppe noticed that when they'd reached the grassy knoll, it was full of people either picnicking or generally lounging about on the grass.

'Won't they be a big problem for us if they're all there in two days' time, boss?' he asked Gabrielli. 'They'll see absolutely everything we're doing.'

'No they won't,' shot back Gabrielli, 'because you and Theo will be dressed as two of Dallas's finest police officers, and you'll move them on, and anyone else hanging around the area, ensuring you keep the shooting line and the angles clear.'

'Oh,' replied Giuseppe. 'Fair enough, boss. No problem then.'

Cavalli had arrived in Dallas, but in all honesty, he hadn't got a clue where to go or what to do. He decided to start by trawling round hotels to see if anyone named Gabrielli had checked in. He got nowhere, because unbeknown to him, Gabrielli and all his team were booked into their hotel under false names, with Jacques having supplied them all with fake ID's he'd acquired via a friend in Chicago whose specialty just happened to be forging dodgy paperwork. After several wasted hours, Cavalli then decided to try a different approach. Not only had he acquired Kennedy's schedule for the next two months, his ex-girlfriend had also given him the route of the President's motorcade through Dallas. He decided to walk the route and see if he could spot anyone. He knew Gabrielli of course, and he also knew Mario, but not Franco, Marco or Giuseppe. He was also totally unaware even of the existence of the six others that had since joined the team.

It's funny how life works out. If Cavalli had decided to walk the route before he had checked out the hotels, then he would have no doubt seen Gabrielli and the others. But alas, by the time he got around to walking the route, Gabrielli had sent all the others back to the hotel while he himself visited a local Dallas nightclub owned by a local man named Jack Ruby.

Gabrielli had been on the lookout for someone like Jack Ruby from the minute he'd arrived in Dallas. He needed someone who worshipped the ground President Kennedy walked on, and was going to be easy to manipulate, particularly if he loaded his drinks with the right drug. Gabrielli's thinking was fairly simple. The only person that knew about Gabrielli and his team and could "drop them in it" was Lee Harvey Oswald. Gabrielli had now convinced Oswald that he had so much confidence in him and his abilities as a marksman that he had decided against using additional gunmen. Oswald didn't know there was going to be another shooter above him firing at JFK, and he truly believed he was now going to be the sole gunman. He also truly believed he'd been asked to do this by the CIA, but nevertheless, he was a danger because he could identify the person who'd gotten him involved, i.e. Gabrielli. So, Oswald had to be gotten rid of as soon as possible after the assassination, but Gabrielli didn't want to risk himself or any of the members of his team.

He knew there would be enormous outrage and anger after the assassination from true Kennedy supporters, and so what he needed was a JFK zealot who would be suitably outraged enough to be prepared to kill the man who had shot his beloved President Kennedy. His first port of call on arriving in Dallas had been the Democrat party headquarters, where he spoke to several people about the impending visit. One of those he had spoken to, who was incredibly excited about Kennedy's visit to Dallas, had been Jack Ruby. From that moment on, he had gone drinking with Ruby at least three times a week, and he used every meeting to get to know him a bit better, to find out what made him tick, and he did and said everything he could to get Ruby even more enthused about how great Kennedy was for the future prosperity and world standing of the USA.

Ruby sucked it all up like a sponge, and by the afternoon of the 20th of November, Gabrielli knew for certain that in a few days' time, with a few drops of the right drug dropped into his drink, it would be enough to send Jack Ruby off, incensed as much as a man can be, to avenge the killing of his beloved President.

Chapter Fifty-One
November 20th, 1963
The White House, Washington D.C.

Jack and Jackie were getting ready for their trip to Dallas. Jack always enjoyed these occasions, as he knew that everywhere he went he would receive riotous applause from the adoring crowds of spectators. Jack absolutely loved it, and he soaked up the adoration, from both the men who wished they were him, and, even better, the women who just wanted him. Jackie, on the other hand, was not quite so keen as her husband. In all honesty, she would rather stay at home with the children, but she would, as usual, do what was expected of the first lady. She would put on a brave face, smile nicely at everyone and say all the right things to every person she met. There were people to do all the packing for them, but Jackie was keen to oversee everything herself, and she wanted to ensure all the clothes she needed on the trip were packed. She'd bought a couple of brand-new outfits, including a rather nice two-piece pink wool suit with blue trim by Chanel, which she thought would be perfect to wear on the motorcade. Jack, as usual, wasn't quite so fussed about his wardrobe, so he just told the team that was doing his packing to load the cases with a selection of his two-piece suits, white shirts and ties; his standard official business attire. Bobby and Ethel, Bobby's wife, despite being invited on the trip by Jack, were not going to Dallas with them as Bobby felt he still had so much to do as U.S. Attorney General, and to his mind, there were far more important things to be doing than sitting in a car waving at crowds, although he fully understood the need for the

President to show his face in public. Besides, Bobby was up to his eyeballs, as he told Jack, in trying to put together a package of policies that would clip the wings of the FBI Director. Feeling much the same as Jack, Bobby really couldn't stand J. Edgar Hoover, he didn't trust J. Edgar Hoover, and if there was one person he'd like to see the back of; it was J. Edgar Hoover.

Gabrielli had decided he found America and Americans very confusing. When he first checked into his hotel, the receptionist asked him, 'How long will you be staying, sir?'

'I'm not completely sure,' he replied, 'but probably about a fortnight.'

'I'm sorry, sir,' she replied, 'a what?'

'A fortnight,' he repeated.

'Again, I'm sorry, sir, but what is a fortnight?'

'It's not a what, it's a how long,' he answered. 'Good grief, woman, it's not complicated; it's simple, basic English,' he said, starting to get annoyed. 'It's an abbreviation of fourteen nights, therefore, a fortnight is two weeks. I thought you people claim to speak English,' he said quite rudely. Gabrielli had learnt to speak his English in England, having spent four extremely productive years in an English public school, or what would be called in America, a private fee-paying school. His family had thought it would be good for him, and that getting what they described as "a superior education" would help him get on in life. The main problem he had now was that as far as he was concerned, Americans claimed to speak English, but for some unknown and totally unfathomable reason, they had decided to change half the words for different ones. Even when they did use the right words, they spelt them differently, or to his mind – incorrectly. Cars were a prime example. The Americans, he annoyingly discovered, call the boot of a car the trunk, and the bonnet was apparently called the hood. Then there was how you fueled a car. Well, that was not only illogical and insane, it was just plain wrong. Gabrielli took great pleasure in explaining it to a bemused Giuseppe.

'Ice, water and steam are all made of H_2O molecules, but what makes them different is that they are perfect examples of the three different forms of basic matter. There are only three: solids, liquids and gases. It's basic chemistry that every kid should learn in school. Now, in Europe, you fuel a car with petrol, and so do the Americans, but for some strange, illogical, unfathomable, crazy and totally incorrect reason, in America, they call petrol gas! Basic chemistry states that there are three different matters, of which gas is one and liquid is another. Petrol, which you use to fuel cars, is a liquid, so why on earth do they call it gas?'

'Yeah, I get it, boss, but then this is America!'

'I know, Giuseppe, but if it's wrong, it's wrong!'

'I guess so, boss,' he replied, not knowing what else to say.

'Then there's the way these Americans spell words. Why, I'd like to know have the Americans removed all the "u"s from words like labor, color, flavor, etc. Is it just laziness, or do they just not know how to spell properly?'

'I've no idea, boss,' answered Giuseppe, still not knowing why Gabrielli had chosen to have his rant at him.

'Well, you used to live here didn't you?' continued Gabrielli. 'Didn't it bother you that they had taken a beautiful language and crucified it beyond recognition?'

'Not really, boss,' he said, floundering for something useful to say. 'Well, I have to say, it upsets me greatly,' said Gabrielli. 'If you're going to use a country's language, the least you should do is treat that language with respect.'

'Yes, boss,' agreed Giuseppe, hoping that was the end of his rant. It was.

After he'd finished his meeting with Jack Ruby, Gabrielli headed to the Texas School Book Depository again and linked up again with Oswald just as he was about to clock off for the day. They chatted outside for a few minutes, and then walked together to Oswald's house. Franco was already there, having parked outside in the car, and on a nod from Gabrielli, he got out of the car, walked to the back and opened the boot, or as he'd discovered over, the last few weeks, the trunk (as the Americans called it). Oswald had been born in 1939, on the 18th of October, to be exact. He'd served in the U.S. military until he was honorably discharged from the Marine Corps, after which he then defected to the Soviet Union where he lived in Minsk where he'd married his wife Marina Nikolayevna Prusakova in 1961. Then, in June 1962, he returned to the USA, bringing his new Russian wife, now called Marina, with him, and they eventually settled down in Dallas. Oswald was only 19 when he decided to travel to Russia, and he'd set off in October 1959, a few days before his 20th birthday. He'd taught himself basic Russian, and he thought he would be very well looked after by the Russians, who would value highly a defecting US military man. They did not, sadly for him, and he ended up with a pretty tedious and very boring job in a Russian factory. After two years, he decided he'd had enough and he headed back to the States with his new wife. Although he felt that communism had let him down personally, he still thought it was a far superior system to anything the USA had on offer, and despite everything, he objected profusely to anyone berating communism. In March 1963, he decided to make his mark. He decided he was going to assassinate a retired U.S. Major General named Edwin Walker, who Oswald considered to be an outspoken anti-communist. Walker had said numerous derogatory comments about the Soviet system, and Oswald decided enough was enough. Walker had to die. For the assassination attempt, he used a second-hand 6.5 mm caliber Carcano rifle he'd bought by mail order for just $29.95 using the bogus name of A. Hidell. On April the 10th, Oswald went by bus to Walker's home one evening, and he was less than a hundred feet away when he shot at the stationery target of Edwin Walker, who was sitting quietly at his desk. Oswald completely missed him, and instead of assassinating the Major General, he just succeeded in destroying the poor man's window frame. Lee Harvey Oswald was, without any shadow of doubt, a totally useless shot and an absolutely terrible marksman. Gabrielli knew all this of course, but he didn't really care. He knew that in Franco, Bernardo and Paulo, he had three really excellent marksmen, each with numerous kills to their names, and anyway, Oswald was simply there to take the blame.

Once they were inside Oswald's home, Franco unwrapped the long brown paper parcel to reveal a brand-new Remington rifle with a telescopic sight attached. He presented it to Oswald as Gabrielli explained to him that the CIA always tried to provide their valuable operatives with the best tools for doing the job. Oswald briefly tried it, but then declared that he preferred his own Carcano rifle as he was more used to it. Gabrielli didn't try to argue with him, and in all honesty, he was quite pleased. It was going to be far better this way, because if Oswald was using his own rifle, it would be one less piece of evidence that could eventually be traced back to them.

After finalizing the exact time and place to meet on the 22nd, they left Oswald's house, taking the Remington hunting rifle and telescopic sight with them. As it turned out, Gabrielli, in fact, never spoke to Oswald again.

Chapter Fifty-Two
November 21st, 1963
Dallas, Texas

Antonio Cavalli woke late after a very restless night; tossing and turning and wondering how on earth he could find Gabrielli and stop him. For a start, he didn't know for sure if the man he was after was actually in Dallas or not. He had no idea of Gabrielli's timetable, and he could only guess at his plans. He tried to think what he would do if he were Gabrielli and he'd been tasked with assassinating the President of the United States. Having thought long and hard about it over two espresso coffees and three cigarettes, he decided he was in the right city, and if it was him, he would try and shoot Kennedy with a hunting rifle from a decent distance giving him the maximum opportunity to escape and live to fight another day. The main question was where exactly. It was already quite a hot day in Dallas, so Cavalli dressed in his favorite light-weight cream-colored linen suit, which he wore over a dark blue shirt. But no tie today, he decided, just for a change. He walked the entire route again, but this time, looking at every building from which he felt a shot could easily be taken in relative safety. After thirty-five to forty minutes of looking at several hotels, numerous apartment blocks, three factories, and goodness knows how many wretched commercial buildings, the last of which just happened to be the Texas School Book Depository, he'd decided there were far too many possibilities. So, he decided to forget that idea.

He decided his next attempt would be to try visiting hotels again, but this time, he would ask the receptionists if there was a group of Italian Americans from out of town staying in the hotel. He felt that way he wasn't giving away any names, and dropping the Holy Office and by association the Pope "in it" so to speak. The first three hotels he tried yielded nothing, but at hotel number four, the receptionist told him yes, there was, in fact, a group of twelve Italian Americans staying. They had taken over the entire twelfth floor. Cavalli felt his luck had changed at last, and so he got into the hotel lift and pushed the button for floor number twelve. The lift stopped and he stepped out onto the smart red and gold plush carpet that lined the hallway. Then, just as the lift doors closed behind him, he was approached by two men wearing white shirts, blue ties and dark blue suits, both with very pronounced bulges in their jackets under their left armpits.

'Can we help you, sir,' asked one of them very politely.

'Yes,' replied Cavalli. 'I'm looking for my good friend Signor Claudio Gabrielli.'

'Sorry, Signor,' replied the bigger of the two men 'there's nobody of that name on this floor. Can we suggest you try another floor or better still, another hotel?'

'Are you sure?' asked Cavalli. 'My friend is...'

He didn't get the chance to finish his question, as the shorter of the two men drew a revolver from under his armpit. He pointed it straight at Cavalli and said, 'Are you deaf, or just plain stupid? Do you have an uncontrollable death wish, my friend? I suggest you do yourself a massive favor and disappear while I'm still in a good mood. If you don't, you may well find you've had a nasty accident involving my gun and a new hole in your head.'

'When Chicago comes visiting Dallas,' interjected the taller one, 'we don't expect to see uninvited visitors, and we certainly don't allow spectators. Do we make ourselves clear or do you need help understanding?'

'I understand completely, sir,' said Cavalli, suddenly realizing that he had gate-crashed a meeting between the main Mafia mobs of Chicago and Dallas. On second thoughts, perhaps simply asking for groups of Italian

Americans at hotels hadn't been such a good idea after all. He decided to apologize to the men, and having done so, he jumped back into the lift immediately after it arrived. Cavalli left the hotel and started walking down the road. He didn't even know where he was exactly, so he looked round for a road sign and discovered he was roughly halfway down somewhere called Dealey Plaza. It looked awfully dull, very tedious and incredibly boring; just a normal dull road with grass on either side in front of a picket fence. Nothing interesting ever happened here, he decided, and so, he continued walking.

Barnardo Bartelli was on the overpass on Dealey Plaza, looking through the telescopic sight he was going to use on his Remington hunting rifle the following day. He was with Franco, Paolo and Mario, who was in charge in Gabrielli's absence, and the four of them were coordinating where and when each of them would shoot. Barnardo was drawn to someone he initially thought looked like a woman in a cream trouser suit, then he realized it was, in fact, a man.

'Look at that stupid idiot dressed in a cream suit,' muttered Barnardo laughing. 'He looks like a bloody Italian ice cream salesman. I ask you, dressed like that in Dallas.' Mario looked where Barnardo was looking and thought he recognized the man. He quickly grabbed the telescopic sight from Barnardo and held it to his eye to make a hundred percent sure.

'That's not an Italian ice cream salesman,' he said. 'That's an ex-Police Inspector who should be in Rome, and certainly not here. Collect your things and let's go.'

Keeping one eye on Cavalli's movements, the four of them climbed into their car. With Barnardo driving, for the rest of the morning, they carried on watching Cavalli from a safe distance as he wandered around Dallas. At lunchtime, he walked back to his hotel, and while he was eating his lunch in the hotel's dining room, Paolo, who Cavalli didn't know and therefore it wouldn't matter if he was seen, checked at the front desk with the hotel's receptionist that Cavalli was, in fact, a guest. Having gotten Cavalli's room number in exchange for a few dollars, he reported back to Mario. Mario immediately decided that Gabrielli needed to know that his deputy had now turned up in the same American city as him. This was definitely no coincidence.

Gabrielli didn't like it; he didn't like it at all. So he decided to take Mario and Franco with him, and go and visit Cavalli in his hotel room. They arrived at the hotel and walked straight past the reception desk without stopping. Fortunately, there was a lift available and they entered and went straight up to Cavalli's floor. They arrived outside his room and knocked on the door, but unbeknown to the three of them, Cavalli had gone out about ten minutes before they'd arrived. Getting no reply, Gabrielli nodded to Mario who took a sliver of thin plastic out of his inside jacket pocket, inserted it in the door and manipulating it, he slipped the lock. The door opened quite quietly and the three of them entered, closing it behind them. Gabrielli had a quick look round the room but found nothing of any interest, so he decided they would sit down and wait for Cavalli's return. He waited nearly two hours, and when Cavalli did get back, Gabrielli was not in the best of moods.

'Where have you been all bloody morning, and more to the point, what the hell are you doing in Dallas?' began Gabrielli. 'I left you in Rome to look after the Holy Office while I was away, so I repeat, what the hell are you doing here in Dallas?'

'I was sent here by the new Holy Father,' replied Cavalli, not in the least bit intimidated by Gabrielli's aggressiveness. After all, he'd been a Police Inspector and he'd faced down far bigger men then Gabrielli. He felt he needed to assert his authority in this situation, so he came straight out with it. 'I have to inform you that you have been suspended from all duties by the Holy Father. I have been put in charge of the Holy Office replacing you, and I have been instructed to tell you to stop your plans regarding President Kennedy immediately, and that you and Signor Orsini here are to return to the Vatican with me and explain your actions to Pope Paul VI.'

'Do you want me to get rid of him, boss?' asked Mario.

'No, just let me think,' Gabrielli replied. Gabrielli remained seated in his chair and thought for a minute or so, during which time Cavalli casually walked over and sat in an armchair, crossing his legs and leaning back in the chair. They were the actions of a man totally in control, not of someone who was feeling just a little bit intimidated.

'On due consideration, I don't think I'll come back to the Vatican with you, Cavalli,' said Gabrielli. 'You say I have been relieved of my position by this new Pope, who I have never even met, so I feel no allegiance to him whatsoever, and besides, the task given to me by the Holy Father I knew and loved, and who set me on this course, is not yet complete.'

'But that is surely the point, Gabrielli,' interrupted Cavalli, 'the new Holy Father doesn't wish you to complete this task. I have spoken at length to the Camerlengo, and he has told me all about your two-stage plan, and what he suspects is stage three. Your presence here in Dallas confirms that his suspicions are correct.'

'You are wasting both my time and yours, Cavalli. Nothing you say will stop what is already set in motion, and so I suggest you leave Dallas and go back to the Vatican. Tell your new master that I shall never return to Rome, but will seek new employment elsewhere once I have completed the task I believe the Holy Father I served would wish me to fulfil. Come Mario, Franco, we are leaving.' With that, Gabrielli got out of his chair, and the three of them left Cavalli's hotel room.

Antonio Cavalli was a very conscientious man, and he was not about to let it go at that. He gave Gabrielli and his two colleagues a minute or two to get down the stairs while he changed into a pair of blue denims, certainly a lot less conspicuous than his cream suit, and then slipped a pale blue jacket over the top. He then ran down the stairs and arrived in the hotel lobby just in time to see the three of them leaving the hotel. They got into a large dark blue Lincoln sedan and drove off. There were always two or three taxis waiting outside the hotel, and Cavalli jumped into the nearest, uttering the words every cab driver the world over longs to hear, 'Follow that car.'

The taxi driver did as had been requested, but he kept well back from the dark blue Lincoln, which eventually came to a halt outside another hotel in central Dallas which Cavalli was unfamiliar with. The three men he was following got out of the car and entered the hotel. Cavalli paid his taxi driver and followed them inside. He watched them all disappear inside the lift which he then watched the arrow on the wall indicator, and it showed the lift, or elevator as these Americans called it, he reminded himself, stopped on the fourth floor. Well, at least he now knew where they were staying, but what could he do to stop the plan Gabrielli had set in motion? He found an armchair in the corner of the lobby, and picked up a newspaper to hide behind if Gabrielli should suddenly appear. He went through, in his mind, the various options open to him. Well, obviously, he could try talking to Gabrielli again, but he knew the man from working under him at the Vatican and he was a hundred percent sure that would achieve nothing. He also realized he couldn't use force as Gabrielli had a team of heavies with him and Cavalli was totally alone. He couldn't call in the Police as at this stage, Gabrielli had done nothing he could arrested for; at least, not as far as he knew.

'OK, so think differently!' How about stopping Kennedy coming to Dallas? But what on earth could he say even if he got through to someone on the telephone? Please don't let the President fly to Dallas, the Vatican has hired a team of hit men to kill him! That would damage the Vatican's reputation forever, and without some kind of proof, he'd just be written off as another crank caller who had some kind of gripe against JFK or worse still, the Pope. The more he thought about it, the more he realized he was in a hopeless position and there was absolutely nothing he could do. He slowly left the lobby and got a taxi back to his own hotel. Perhaps a brandy and an afternoon siesta would help inspire him, but he doubted it.

Once back in his hotel suite, Gabrielli sat down with Mario, while Franco went to get Giuseppe and Marco. Once the original five of them were all together, he explained the current situation and told them, as far as he was concerned, nothing had changed.

'I have never met this new Pope,' he began, 'and I certainly have no intention of following his wishes over those of the previous Pope who I have always served and loved to the end. We have no definite way of knowing if he would have authorized stage three of the plan as he sadly passed away before I could get his permission to proceed. But it is my firm belief that he would have, without doubt, said yes, as it is the only way of stopping Kennedy from bringing the name and reputation of the Roman Catholic Church into disrepute, and causing long-lasting damage that would take decades to repair. Of this, I have no doubt.'

'Well, I know nothing about all of that, boss,' said Franco. 'But I think I speak for all of us when I say that doesn't matter to us. We work for you and we do what you tell us. It makes no difference to us where your orders come from. Our loyalty is to you and it always will be.'

'Here, here,' said Giuseppe as the others all nodded their heads.

'Well, thank you, boys,' said Gabrielli. 'That is indeed good to know. I don't think we need to tell any of the others about any of this. As for your own situation, well, I have to tell you that over the last few years, and unbeknown to the Vatican, I have managed to set up several secret bank accounts around the world with enough of the Vatican's money salted away in all of them that will keep the five of us in relative wealth for as long as we live. So don't worry about getting paid. Nothing changes.'

'Any changes to the plan, boss?' asked Mario.

'None at all,' he answered. 'Tomorrow afternoon, John Fitzgerald Kennedy, the President of the United States, dies.'

Chapter Fifty-Three
November 22nd, 1963
Dallas, Texas

The morning of Friday the 22nd of November, 1963 saw ten new Police officers on the streets of Dallas. Unfortunately, the Dallas Police Department was totally unaware of their existence. Those ten new officers in their freshly laundered and dry-cleaned uniforms were Bernardo Bartelli, Paolo Calico, Jacques Deangelo, Rafael Patressi, Theodore Silvestri, Salvador Mascolla, Giuseppe Mancuso, Franco Lamberti, Mario Orsini and Marco Farina. Looking just as smart in a dark blue three-piece pinstriped suit was Signor Claudio Gabrielli, and all eleven of them left their hotel to head for three different locations. Franco and Salvador took the Pontiac and drove to the rear of the Texas School Book Depository where they dumped the car, deliberately leaving the keys in the ignition where some helpful thief would probably steal it. It would never be used by any of them ever again. Franco and Salvador then headed for the rear entrance of the building, with Franco's hunting rifle sitting neatly in its smart wooden case strung over his shoulder by a leather strap. Bernardo, the second gunman, and Marco, along with Gabrielli himself, took the Lincoln and headed for the railway overpass. Again, they dumped the car a couple of streets away leaving the keys in the ignition. The rest of the team, including Paolo, the third gunmen, had stolen a large plain gray-colored van from outside a baker's shop and they drove to a disused piece of waste ground where they also dumped their vehicle. Getting out of the van, they all headed to the grassy knoll. They all had their specific jobs to do, and each man knew exactly what was expected of him. Salvador's main task was to ensure Franco got free and undisturbed access to the seventh floor of the Book Depository, and once Franco was set up, his main task was to stop anyone who wanted to stop Franco. They were in luck, as nobody saw them slip in through a back door, using a key Oswald had supplied to them several days earlier, having had a copy cut for them from his own official key given to him as an employee of the book depository. All was quiet, and they slowly climbed the stairs. Once settled in position, Franco screwed together the various sections of his Remington hunting rifle, attached the telescopic sight, which had been previously synchronized with the rifle in the woods a few days earlier, and then he neatly laid out four bullets, ready to grab them instantaneously. Franco settled down and began reading that morning's newspaper. He was extremely calm, as he always was in these situations, and this was just another day's work, similar to many other days he'd had. It was his calm and relaxed attitude Gabrielli believed that made him so good at what he did. Having seen him set up and ready to go, Salvador walked down one flight of stairs to the sixth floor where he was highly relieved to find Lee Harvey Oswald. He wasn't quite so calm. But Salvador spent time with him, telling him how important he was, and that what he was going to be doing today was a service to the world in getting rid of this dangerous President. He did everything he could to help Oswald relax, and he'd even brought him a flask of hot, sweet tea which Oswald gratefully accepted, commenting to Salvador that "the CIA obviously leaves nothing to chance". Salvador just smiled at him. Once Oswald was settled, Salvador went down another floor to the fifth, and took up his own position on the staircase where he alone could control access to both the sixth and seventh floors until it was all over, and the job was done.

Paolo would be the second gunman to fire, but he was, without doubt, going to be the most exposed being located behind the picket fence on the grassy knoll. So Jacques, Mario, Marco and Giuseppe all arrived at the area in front of the fence, and once Paolo had shown them exactly where he wanted to be set up, and what area he needed kept clear for his line of sight, their job was to keep people away from that area until the motorcade had passed. Theo and Rafael we're behind the picket fence with Paolo, and their job was to keep everyone away from Paolo. It was amazing, thought Giuseppe, how people just accepted that they were all legitimate police officers. But then again, why wouldn't they? They were all wearing genuine police uniforms and they were simply keeping the area clear in preparation for the Presidential drive through.

Up on the railway overpass, Gabrielli was standing next to Bernardo and Marco, who were both dressed in their police uniforms. Gabrielli himself had a shiny Dallas Police Captain's gold badge clipped over his jacket top pocket that Raphael had stolen four days earlier from the dressing room of the showers where Captain Peter Sanchez freshened up at the end of each day's shift. He'd patiently followed him for three consecutive evenings, learning his routines and getting to know how long he spent in the shower, and he then stole his badge on the fourth. Gabrielli took his radio out of his briefcase, pulled the aerial to its full height, and called round to his troops in order. Franco was first, and he confirmed he was in position, ready, waiting and bored out of his brain having now read through the newspaper twice. Gabrielli laughed and casually suggested he read it a third time. He really wasn't worried about Franco. He was the best gunman he knew and he'd used him on numerous occasions before, and every one had been completely successful. Paolo was also ready and waiting, as was Mario, whose task was to ensure Paolo had a clear sight line by keeping a specific area of the grassy knoll in front of the picket fence completely clear. He was allowing one or two folks to take up position right at the front, but that was where the grassy knoll sloped down, and that was OK because Paolo would be shooting well over their heads. Like Franco and Paolo, Bernardo had his weapon primed and ready, but in all honesty, Gabrielli was hoping the job would be done before the motorcade reached the overpass.

Bernardo's rifle was leaning against a concrete pillar on the overpass, but it had a dark blue police towel draped over it, also acquired by Raphael from the showers. It not only hid the weapon from sight, it kept dust and anything else from entering the barrel. Shooters and marksmen the world over are all the same. They are very particular about keeping their weapons clean.

Jack and Jackie's motorcade route through Dallas that day had been carefully planned to give Jack the maximum amount of exposure to the local crowds prior to his arrival for a lunch at the Trade Mart, where he would meet with both civic and business leaders. The White House staff had informed the Secret Service that the President would arrive at Dallas Love Field via a short flight from Carswell Air Force Base in Fort Worth.

The Dallas Trade Mart had been preliminarily selected for the lunch, and Kenneth O'Donnell, Jack's friend and his appointment's secretary, had selected the Trade Mart as the final destination on the motorcade route. Leaving from Dallas Love Field, the motorcade had been allotted 45 minutes to reach the Trade Mart at a planned arrival time of 12.15 p.m. The itinerary was designed to be a meandering 10-mile route between the two locations, and that meant the parade route vehicles could be driven reasonably slowly to give the crowds a chance to see Jack and Jackie properly. But even so, they would hopefully still arrive for lunch at the allotted time. Special Agent Winston Lawson, a member of the White House detail who acted as the advance Secret Service Agent, and Secret Service Agent Forrest Sorrels, the Special Agent in charge of the Dallas office, were the two agents that had planned the actual route. On November 14th, both men attended a meeting at Love Field and drove over the route that Sorrels believed was the best suited for the motorcade. From Love Field, the route passed through a suburban portion of Dallas, then it went through downtown along Main Street, and finally to the Trade Mart via a short segment of the Stemmons Freeway. Gabrielli had been both thrilled and amazed to see the planned route being widely reported in Dallas newspapers several days before the event. As far as the newspapers were concerned, publishing the route was for the benefit of all the people who wished to view the motorcade. As far as Gabrielli was concerned, publishing the route was for the benefit of him personally, as it helped him enormously in carefully planning Kennedy's assassination. In order to pass through Downtown Dallas, a route west along Dallas' Main Street, rather than Elm Street (one block to the north) was chosen, because this had always been the traditional parade route, and it also provided the maximum views for people from surrounding buildings. It allowed numerous places for crowds to gather and view the motorcade. The route on Main Street precluded a direct turn onto the Fort Worth Turnpike exit (which served also as the Stemmons Freeway exit), which was the route to the Trade Mart, because this exit was only accessible from Elm Street. The planned motorcade route therefore had to include a short one-block turn at the end of the downtown segment of Main Street, onto Houston Street for one block northward, before turning again west onto Elm, in order to proceed through Dealey Plaza before exiting Elm onto the Stemmons Freeway. The Texas School Book Depository was conveniently situated at the northwest corner of Houston and Elm. Three vehicles were eventually used for Secret Service and police protection in the motorcade. The first car, an unmarked white Ford sedan, carried Dallas Police Chief Jesse Curry, Secret Service Agent Winston Lawson, Sheriff Bill Decker and Dallas Field Agent Forrest Sorrels. The second car, a 1961 Lincoln Continental convertible, was occupied by the driver, Agent Bill Greer and SAIC Roy Kellerman in the front, Governor John Connally and his wife Nellie Connally sitting behind them, and in the back row and slightly raised so that the crowds could see them clearly, the President and Mrs. Kennedy. The third car, a 1955 Cadillac convertible contained the driver, Agent Sam Kinney, ATSAIC Emory Roberts, presidential aides Ken O'Donnell and Dave Powers, driver Agent George Hickey and PRS agent Glen Bennett. Four Secret Service agents; Clint Hill, Jack Ready, Tim McIntyre and Paul Landis rode on the running boards. On November the 22nd, after a breakfast speech in Fort Worth, where Jack had stayed overnight having arrived from San Antonio, Houston, and Washington D.C. the previous day, he boarded Air Force One, which departed at 11:10 and arrived at Love Field 15 minutes later. At about 11:40, the presidential motorcade, having been previously assembled, left Love Field for the trip through Dallas, running on a schedule about 10 minutes longer than the original planned 45, due to very enthusiastic crowds estimated at between 150,000 and 200,000 people. There had, in addition, been two unplanned stops directed by Jack, which had also put them a bit behind schedule. By the time they had reached Dealey Plaza, they were only five minutes away from their planned destination.

When Jack's open top Lincoln Continental convertible entered Dealey Plaza at 12.30 p.m. Franco had already been in his firing position on the seventh floor of the book depository for well over an hour, just to be on the safe side. He had the window half-open, enough to give him a clear shot, but also keeping it partly closed gave him added protection should anyone happen to look in his direction. He was positioned about four feet back from the window inside the room, again making him impossible to see for anyone who happened for any reason to be looking in his direction. The Remington hunting rifle had been very carefully assembled with its telescopic sight, and checked over three times to ensure everything was perfect. The barrel was firmly attached to a very strong and professional tripod about six inches from its business end as Franco referred to it, ensuring steadiness, and also removing any weight in lifting the weapon. In order to get the right angle, he would have to be standing rather than sitting or lying down, but he preferred that anyway. Franco was every inch the professional, even down to the black rubber-soled shoes he was wearing which ensured his feet wouldn't slip on the floor at the critical moment. He had also checked twice via Salvador that Oswald was also in position and ready to shoot from his position, one floor below him on the sixth.

As the three cars entered Dealey Plaza, Nellie Connally, the First Lady of Texas, turned around to Jack, who was sitting immediately behind her, and said, 'Mr. President, you can't say Dallas doesn't love you,' which Jack acknowledged by saying,

'No, you certainly can't.'

Those were the last four words ever spoken by President John F. Kennedy.

From Houston Street, the presidential limousine made the planned left turn onto Elm Street, allowing it access to the Stemmons Freeway exit. As the vehicle turned onto Elm, the motorcade passed the Texas School Book Depository. At that point, Franco heard a gunshot from below him, and he knew straight away that Oswald had fired his first shot. There was very little reaction from Jack's car other than some head turning to see where the noise had come from. It was obvious to Franco that Oswald was repeating the same level of incompetence that he had shown against retired Major General Edwin Walker i.e. once again he had completely missed the target.

'Useless bloody idiot,' muttered Franco to nobody in particular, and immediately after he'd spoken, he gently squeezed the trigger and fired his own weapon. Within a second of each other, Jack, Jackie and Governor Connally had all turned their heads abruptly from looking to their left to looking to their right, all three of them having heard Oswald's first shot, and recognizing it for what it was. Seeing that nobody had been hit, Connally then turned his head and torso to his right, attempting to see President Kennedy behind him. He could not see Jack, so he then started to turn forward again, turning from his right to his left. It was at this precise moment that Franco fired. When Connally's head was facing roughly 20 degrees left of center, he was hit in his upper right back by Franco's first bullet.

Franco's first shot had, in fact, hit Jack first, who had reacted by raising his arms and elbows, with his hands in front of his face and throat, but the bullet had gone straight through him and passed into Connally's back. Jackie, realizing what had happened, immediately cradled her husband in her arms, but at that point, Franco, who thought his first shot had missed Jack and had only hit John Connally, cursed, took careful aim again, and having quickly reloaded, he once more gently squeezed the trigger. Back in the car, Nellie Connally who had now heard the second gunshot, Franco's first, and then Governor Connally yelling, turned away from Jack toward her husband, at which point she heard another gunshot; Franco's second. Suddenly she, Jackie and the limousine's rear interior were covered with fragments of Jack's skull, his blood, and his brain. Unbeknown to anyone in the three cars, and more by luck than judgment, Paolo had fired his first shot from the Grassy Knoll at the exact precise same moment as Franco had fired his second, and so it sounded to everyone like a single shot. He too had hit Jack's head. The impact of two bullets passing through the same area of Jack's head at the same time meant instant death, and Jack, thankfully, wouldn't have felt a thing. However, the effect was horrifying to witness and totally devastating as Jack's blood and fragments of his scalp, brain, and skull not only landed on the interior of the car, but also on the inner and outer surfaces of the front glass windshield, the raised sun visors, as well as on the front engine hood and the rear trunk lid. His blood and skull fragments also landed on the follow-up Secret Service car and its driver's left arm, as well as on the motorcycle officers who were riding on both sides of the President just behind his vehicle. Secret Service Special Agent Clint Hill, was riding on the left front running board of the follow-up car, which was immediately behind the Presidential limousine. When he heard the shooting start, he jumped off the running board and ran forward to try to get on the limousine and protect the President, but he never made it in time. After Jack had been shot in the head, Jackie began to climb out onto the back of the limousine, and Clint Hill thought she was reaching for a piece of the President's shattered skull she'd seen. He jumped onto the back of the limousine while at the same time, Jackie returned to her seat, and he clung hard to the car as it exited

Dealey Plaza and accelerated away, speeding to Parkland Memorial Hospital.

From his elevated position on the flyover, Bernardo and Gabrielli had seen everything, and they could both clearly see that Jack was already dead. Gabrielli reached out towards Bernardo's rifle, put his hand on the barrel and gently pushed it downwards, indicating that there was no need for him to fire. He did so with satisfaction at a job well done. All Gabrielli needed to do now was ensure someone else got the blame.

After a highly distraught Jackie had crawled back into her limousine seat, not having a clue what to do and feeling utterly useless as well as shocked, both Governor Connally and Mrs. Connally heard her say, 'They have killed my husband; I have his brains in my hand.'

Antonio Cavalli had got up that fateful morning not sure what the hell he could do, if anything, and in the end, he'd decided to go and watch the motorcade pass by, and with any luck he might see Gabrielli or Mario, the only two he knew by sight. He ended up, purely by chance, standing next to a man he'd never seen before named James Tague, and with mounting shock and complete horror, they both stood there watching the horrific events taking place on Dealey Plaza. Halfway through the shooting, Tague suddenly felt a nasty sting on his right cheek from what turned out to be a bit of broken bullet casing from Oswald's second shot. FBI and Dallas Police investigations later stated that Tague had been standing 531 feet away from the Texas Book Depository's sixth floor easternmost window, and that he was more than 16 feet below the top of where the President's head would have been. In other words, and not to put too fine a point on it, Lee Harvey Oswald's second shot was just like his first; a complete miss. His second shot was over 16 feet off target, proving yet again that he was certainly no great shot, but as sure as hell – he was going to make a great patsy. The Dallas Police later confirmed that there were a total of 104 eyewitnesses in Dealey Plaza that afternoon, all of whom were later put on record as to their opinion on which direction the shots had come from. 54 of them thought that the shots had come from the direction of the Texas School Book Depository. 33 of them thought that the shots had come from the area of the grassy knoll, and the remaining 17 thought that the shots had come from both directions. As it happens, they were all correct.

Chapter Fifty-Four
November 22nd, 1963
Dallas, Texas

After Franco had fired his second and fatal shot, he knew he'd done his job properly and successfully, so he quickly undid the thumbscrew holding the telescopic sight in place, and then put both the sight and the hunting rifle in its wooden case, closed it and locked it. He quietly walked down a single flight of stairs to the sixth floor where he found Oswald, trying unsuccessfully to load another bullet into his bolt-action rifle.

'Forget it, Lee,' he said encouragingly, 'you've done your job and Kennedy's well and truly dead. Very well done, by the way; that was really nice shooting. The most important thing now is that you get away from here, and quick.' Oswald started to pack up the Carcano rifle to take it with him, but Franco stopped him. He needed the evidence left where it was by the window on the sixth floor.

'Leave it, Lee, leave everything here, it doesn't matter. Nobody will know who shot him even if they did find the rifle, but they won't because we'll take it with us and dispose of it. Just get yourself out of here. Go to that cinema we talked about before and watch the film. It will help calm your nerves, and let's face it, Lee, who the hell would dream of looking for Kennedy's killer in a movie theatre? Now go on, go, we'll clear up here, and don't let anyone stop you.'

'Thanks, George,' he said, using the bogus name Franco had given him weeks earlier. 'You've been really great.'

After Oswald had left and run down the stairs, Franco and Sal very carefully hid and covered his rifle with cardboard boxes, but they made sure it was only partially hidden, and that enough of it was showing for it to be easily discovered. He then casually and slowly descended down the rear stairwell himself, not bothered about being seen as he was dressed in a Dallas Police officer's uniform, and he'd also now applied a false brown moustache Jacques had given him that morning.

About a minute or so later, Oswald was passing through the second-floor lunchroom, on his way out of the building when he ran into police officer Marrion L. Baker who had his gun drawn. Fortunately for Oswald, the patrolman was accompanied by a Texas Book Depository employee and Oswald's own supervisor, Roy Truly. Baker sadly made the mistake of letting Oswald pass after Truly had identified him as an employee. Baker and Truly had incorrectly assumed that Oswald was not a suspect just because he was an employee of the building. According to Baker when he was later interviewed, he said, 'Oswald did not appear to be nervous or out of breath.' The next person Lee Harvey Oswald ran into was a clerical assistant working at the Texas Book Depository named Mrs. Robert Reid, who had returned to her office within two minutes of the shooting. Oswald had now picked up and opened a bottle of coke from the lunchroom, which he was guzzling down, and he had also managed to calm down quite a bit. As Mrs. Reid walked past him, she simply told him, 'The President has been shot.'

Oswald, not wanting to be delayed in getting away, simply mumbled something totally incoherent in response, but Mrs. Reid did not understand what he'd said. Oswald then continued to head for the way out and he just about made it through the front door before the Dallas police sealed it off. Franco and Salvador had already made their own escape, climbing out through a ground floor window at the back of the building, taking their weapons with them. Oswald's rifle they had deliberately left behind to be found by the police. As soon as he was clear of the building and out of public view, Franco pulled up the aerial and radioed Gabrielli.

'All clear, boss,' he said, smiling. 'Time to make your telephone call.'

'Thanks, Franco,' he replied, 'and well done.'

Gabrielli had already moved from the railway overpass to a public telephone box, where he had been waiting to receive Franco's radio call. As soon as he'd received it, he picked up the telephone, dialed the number he'd already gotten written down for the Dallas Police Station he knew would be nearest to Oswald's new location, assuming, of course, Oswald had stuck to their plan. Gabrielli then gave the police a highly convincing story of how he had seen shots coming from what looked like either the fifth or sixth floor of the Texas Book Depository. He then went on to describe how a couple of minutes later, he saw this man come running out of the same building looking highly suspicious. Gabrielli then described Lee Harvey Oswald in great detail, but obviously without using any names, including his own.

At about 12.40 pm Oswald boarded a city bus, but due to the heavy traffic he got off just two blocks later. Oswald, who was in a hurry, then took a local taxi to his rooming house at 1026 North Beckley Avenue, and he eventually went in through the front door at around 1.00 pm. He was in the rooming house because his Russian wife had walked out on him and told him she'd had enough and wanted a divorce. He'd told her to stay at the house and he'd move out, so she stayed and he moved to North Beckley Avenue. Although he saw his housekeeper, Earlene Roberts, when he arrived, Oswald never spoke to her, and he just dived straight into his room and slammed the door behind him. A few minutes later, he left the room, zipping up a jacket he'd now put on, which covered a handgun he'd also picked up from his room. After Oswald had left, Mrs. Roberts looked out of the window of her house and saw him standing at the northbound Beckley Avenue bus stop in front of her house.

At roughly 1.15 pm, a Dallas patrolman named J. P. Tippit drove up in his patrol car, and stopped alongside Oswald as he was walking down the street. Tippit thought Oswald resembled the police broadcast description of the man that had been described in the anonymous phone call they'd received from Gabrielli. Oswald, who by now was about a mile from his boarding house, was asked to stop by Officer Tippit and stand still as he wanted to question him. Oswald thought he was about to be arrested for killing the President, and so without thinking twice, he simply reached inside his jacket, pulled out his handgun, fired it straight at Officer Tippit and killed the policeman with four quick shots. Numerous witnesses heard the shots and then saw Oswald run off as fast as he could, still holding the revolver. Unbeknown to him, the manager of a shoe store named Johnny Brewer had also seen what had happened, and he watched Oswald duck into the entrance alcove of his store. Not being sure what to do, and not wanting to get himself shot, Brewer did nothing to try and stop him, but he did continue to watch Oswald as he then left the alcove and hurriedly continued up the street. Like the great patsy he was, Lee Harvey Oswald was doing exactly as Franco had suggested to him earlier, and he slipped into the nearby cinema, the Texas Theatre, where they were showing a new film entitled "Cry of Battle".

Gabrielli, who by now had made his way to the outside of the theatre, was casually watching events unfold from the other side of the road. He decided to give Oswald five minutes to get settled, and then he'd ring the police again and make his second anonymous call of the day. However, he never got to make that second call as unbeknown to Gabrielli, Brewer had already alerted the theatre's ticket clerk, and they had then telephoned the police at approximately 1:40 p.m. As the police arrived, the house lights in the cinema were brought up and Brewer, who was now with the police, went into the theatre with them and pointed out Oswald, who was sitting near the rear of the theatre. Police Officer Nick McDonald was the first to reach Oswald, who looked up at him, then appearing to be totally deflated and giving himself up he said, 'Well, it is all over now.' But, as he was speaking, Oswald pulled out his handgun which he had tucked into the front of his trousers. He pointed it at Officer McDonald who, realizing he was about to be killed, grabbed for the gun, and fortunately for him, the gun's hammer came down on the webbing between his thumb and index finger when Oswald pulled the trigger. Realizing he was now in big trouble, Oswald struck out at the officer, but McDonald hit him back and Oswald was soon disarmed as several other police officers arrived to help their colleague. As Lee Harvey Oswald was led from the theatre, he started shouting that he'd done nothing wrong, and that he was yet another victim of police brutality. Gabrielli, who had slipped into the theatre after the police to watch what was happening, stood quietly in the shadows and smiled to himself. He quietly left the building two minutes after Oswald's arrest.

Around 2:00 pm, Oswald was taken to the Dallas Police Department building, where homicide detective Jim Leavelle questioned him about the murder of Officer Tippit. When Captain J. W. Fritz heard Oswald's name being mentioned, he recognized it as being the name of the Texas Book Depository employee who had been reported missing, and was wanted as a major suspect in the assassination of the President. Oswald was formally charged with the murder of Officer Tippit at 7.10 pm that same evening, and eventually at around 1.30 am the next morning, Lee Harvey Oswald was also charged with the assassination of President John Fitzgerald Kennedy.

Soon after his arrest, Oswald encountered several reporters in the hallway of the police building where he declared to them, 'I didn't shoot anybody. They've taken me in because of the fact that I lived in the Soviet Union. I'm just a patsy.' Well, he was certainly right on the last point.

Later, at an arranged press meeting, one of the numerous reporters present asked Oswald, 'Did you kill the President?'

Oswald, who at that particular moment in time had only been charged with murdering Officer Tippit, but had not yet been charged with Kennedy's death answered, 'No, I have not been charged with that. In fact, nobody has said that to me yet. The first thing I heard about it was when the newspaper reporters in the hall asked me that question.'

As he was then being led from the room one of the reporters called out, 'What did you do in Russia, and how did you hurt your eye?'

'A policeman hit me,' Oswald replied.

Chapter Fifty-Five
November 24th, 1963
Dallas, Texas

Gabrielli sat quietly in his hotel suite and went through in his mind again, everything he knew about Jack Ruby, and thought through yet again how best to manipulate him into doing what he needed done. He'd spent most of the previous evening drinking with Ruby at his club, telling him how Oswald was incredibly anti-Semitic, and how he despised everything Kennedy had been trying to do for the country. He'd now given him over 24 hours to work himself up over Kennedy's assassination, and he was positive it was now time for the final act.

Ruby was actually born Jacob Leon Rubenstein on March 25, 1911, in Chicago. He was the son of Joseph Rubenstein and Fannie Turek Rutkowski who were both Polish-born Orthodox Jews. Ruby was the fifth of his parents' ten surviving children and he grew up in the Maxwell Street area of Chicago. He had quite a troubled childhood and a lousy adolescence marked by frequent juvenile delinquency, and he consequently spent a lot of time in foster homes. At the age of just 11, he was arrested for truancy, and he eventually skipped school so many times that he ended up spending time at the Institute for Juvenile Research. Still a relatively young man, he sold horse-racing tip sheets and various novelties, and then acted as a business agent for the local refuse collector's union that eventually became part of the International Brotherhood of Teamsters.

From his quite early childhood, Ruby had been nicknamed 'Sparky' by those who knew him. According to his sister, Eva Grant, he acquired the nickname because he resembled a slow-moving horse named "Sparky" in the contemporary comic strip "Barney Google", although a couple of drinking acquaintances told Gabrielli the nickname was directly connected with his quick temper. In either event, Ruby didn't like the nickname Sparky and he was quick to fight anyone who called him that. Gabrielli had made a quick note on a pad – "Got a quick temper and easy to wind up".

In the 1940s, Ruby frequented racetracks in both Illinois and California. Drafted in 1943, he then served in the U.S. Army Air Forces during World War II, working as an aircraft mechanic at U.S. bases until 1946. He had an honorable record and was promoted to Private First Class. Upon his discharge on February 21st, 1946, he returned to Chicago.

The following year, Ruby finally moved to Dallas where both he and his brothers soon shortened their surnames from Rubenstein to Ruby. Hopefully, they hoped, removing any Jewish connotations, although he told Gabrielli during one of their many drinking sessions that it was simply because the name "Rubenstein" was too long and anyway, he was really well known as Jack Ruby. Ruby managed various nightclubs, strip clubs, and dance halls, through which he had developed close ties to many Dallas Police officers who frequented his nightclubs, where he happily provided them with free liquor, free prostitutes and other favors. He told Gabrielli it was well worth it and bound to be good for him in the long run if and when he needed a favor from the police. Gabrielli made a note of that as well. Finally, he wrote on his pad that Ruby had never married, nor did he have any children.

It was Gabrielli's clear impression from their numerous conversations that Jack Ruby was quite heavily involved in the underworld activities of illegal gambling, narcotics, and prostitution. Gabrielli didn't know it, but in 1956, an FBI report had stated that their informant, a woman named Eileen Curry reported that in January of that year, she'd moved to Dallas with her boyfriend, James Breen, after jumping bond on narcotics charges. Breen told her that he had made connections with a large narcotics setup operating between Texas, Mexico, and the East and that James had been given the OK to operate from a Jack Ruby of Dallas.

Now, 24 hours after the assassination, Gabrielli headed to Ruby's "Carousel Club" which was located at 1312 1/2 Commerce Street in downtown Dallas. Ruby had told him the previous evening that he was in the second-floor advertizing offices of the *Dallas Morning News*, five blocks away from the Texas School Book Depository, placing his weekly advertisements for his nightclubs when he'd learned of the terrible assassination, and that had been around 12:45 p.m. Ruby then made a couple of phone calls to his assistant at the Carousel Club and to his sister, telling them the dreadful news that he'd just heard.

Ruby decided he wanted to see what this Oswald character looked like, and he had been seen in the halls of the Dallas Police Headquarters on several occasions after Lee Harvey Oswald's arrest on November 22nd. Unbeknown to him, there was even newsreel footage from WFAA-TV (Dallas) and NBC showing that Ruby had gone there impersonating a newspaper reporter during a press conference at Dallas Police Headquarters on the night of Kennedy's death.

It was now November 24th, and Gabrielli met briefly with Ruby one last time and told him he had just heard from a reliable source that Oswald might now get away with killing the President, as his defense lawyer was claiming nobody saw him do it, and therefore there was no real evidence, just a rifle which could have been used by anyone. Gabrielli kept verbally pushing and pulling him, telling him Oswald was likely to walk, and even suggesting someone should do something about it. He made sure Ruby was really incensed, then he dropped a small amount of a clear liquid drug into his drink that would make him extremely hyperactive. Then he watched him drive off into town with one of his pet dogs. Ruby sent an emergency money order at the Western Union on Main Street to one of his employees at 11.17 am, and then he walked one-half block to the nearby Dallas police headquarters. He made his way into the basement via a stairway accessible from an alleyway next to the Dallas Municipal Building. At 11.21 am, while authorities were escorting Oswald through the police basement to an armored car that was to take him to the nearby county jail, Ruby now totally incensed that this creep, as he thought of Oswald, might get away with it, stepped out from a crowd of reporters and fired a single round from his revolver into Oswald's abdomen, fatally wounding him.

Ruby was immediately subdued by both agents and police. The shooting was broadcast live nationally, and millions of television viewers witnessed it. Oswald was taken by ambulance while unconscious to Parkland Memorial Hospital, which, as it happened, was the self-same hospital where doctors had tried to save President Kennedy's life two days earlier. They failed again, and Oswald died at 1:07 p.m.

Gabrielli returned to his hotel suite, where, to his great surprise, he found Antonio Cavalli waiting for him sitting in an armchair. Cavalli also knew how to get into people's hotel rooms uninvited.

'And to what do I owe the pleasure of your company?' asked Gabrielli.

'I just thought it would be good to have a chat before I return to the Vatican.'

'And what exactly, may I ask, did you want to chat about?' asked Gabrielli.

'Please assure me you and your team had nothing to do with the assassination of President Kennedy.'

'If it helps your peace of mind, I will assure you I had nothing to do with it.'

'I don't want peace of mind Gabrielli, I want the truth,' said Cavalli.

'Then you need to ask better questions,' replied Gabrielli smiling. 'Of course we did it, and you already knew that or you wouldn't be here. Now, what do you really want?'

'I want to be sure this doesn't end up being placed at the Vatican's front door. This is down to you Gabrielli, and it has nothing to do with the Vatican.'

'That's total crap, Cavalli, and you know it. This whole thing was started by Pope John XXIII. It was his commission and he was totally aware of every aspect of the three-stage plan I put together.'

'But surely you realized the whole thing had to stop the minute he died and Pope Paul VI was chosen as the new Pope. Surely your commission ended with Pope John's death.'

'My commission ended when the Holy Father's wishes were completed,' stated Gabrielli.

'But the Holy Father is the current Pope, Gabrielli, not the dead man who gave you a totally reckless commission which you should never have accepted.'

'Look, Cavalli, let me make this clear. As far as I am concerned, your wonderful President Kennedy was a dirty, womanizing, uncontrollable shit who treated his poor wife and children appallingly, and acted as if they were totally irrelevant to his life. As the President of the most powerful nation on earth, his lifestyle was, without doubt, going to bring the Catholic Church into disrepute and crap all over everything the Holy Father stood for. He had to be stopped.'

'But assassination?' asked Cavalli.

'We'd tried everything else. Bishop O'Boyle had a meeting with him in the Oval Office and told him in no uncertain terms that the Holy Father expected him to change his ways now he was President. His response was incredibly arrogant, and in effect, he threw the Bishop out of the White House.'

'Not a helpful response, I admit,' mused a thoughtful Cavalli.

'We also spoke to as many of his women as we could and warned them off. Several were scared and ended their relationship with him, but others refused.'

'And what, may I ask, happened to them?' asked Cavalli.

'Let's just say they were dealt with,' answered Gabrielli.

'That's no answer.'

'I promise you, you really don't want to know,' he said. 'Look, we did what had to be done in order for the Holy Father's wishes to be completed. As for the changes at the

Vatican, well, for a start I've never even met this new Pope, and I've certainly never spoken to him, and yet he decides to sack me and then he gives you my job. I owe him nothing.'

'I'm sorry, Gabrielli, I understand this must seem greatly unfair to you, but I have to ask you to guarantee me that this will not come back to haunt the Vatican.'

'Why should it?' he responded. 'The man who started all this has sadly passed away, and I suppose, if I'm totally honest, he was totally unaware of my final decision to see it through to the end, and yes, in all fairness to the Vatican, as he never gave me the final go ahead, you could say this was, in the end, all down to me. But make no mistake, Cavalli, it was the Vatican that started all this. As for me and my team, well, we'll all be returning to what we know best, and that certainly won't be in Rome. Fear not, Cavalli, your precious new Pope is safe from anything that might be aimed at the Vatican.'

'And I have your word on that?'

'You do. We are not amateurs Cavalli, and we were incredibly careful with every aspect of every stage of what we did. One of the key elements of my plan was to make sure someone else got the blame, which I think we managed to do very successfully. All I have left to say now is goodbye, Signor Cavalli, and I am absolutely positive our paths will never cross again. Oh, and good luck in your new job; I think you'll need it.'

With that, Cavalli stood up, and as he was about to leave, Gabrielli offered him a handshake. He thought of declining, but decided it would be best to part on peaceful terms. He made his way back to his own hotel, had a long shower, packed his bags and then headed for the airport and the next available flight to Rome and his wife.

Epilogue

'Please assure me, Signor Cavalli,' began Pope Paul, 'that the Vatican played no part in the assassination of President Kennedy.'

'I will do my best, Holy Father, but sadly we do not have all the answers. We know that Pope John XXIII commissioned an extensive report into the life of President Kennedy as he was extremely concerned about the late President's morals, with him being a married man, and yet, having frequent adulterous affairs with women other than his wife. The Holy Father felt this was far from being the right moral example to be set by such a prominent Roman Catholic as the President of the United States, and he did not wish for such behavior to become public knowledge and reflect badly on the church.'

'That, I can easily understand,' acknowledged the Pope.

'However,' continued Cavalli 'as far as we know, you now possess the only remaining copy of that report which you have placed in the Vatican archives, with a papal denial seal on it i.e., it will never see the light of day unless a future pope reverses your decision, which would be highly unlikely. We also know that the Holy Father asked Bishop O'Boyle to speak to the President and that the resulting meeting at the Oval Office did not go well. All of this can be confirmed by both the Bishop himself and the Camerlengo, who was present when Bishop O'Boyle reported back to the Holy Father on the result of his disastrous meeting with President Kennedy. We also know that the Holy Father then asked to see Signor Gabrielli in private, and as a result of that meeting, Gabrielli, along with several colleagues, all travelled to the United States. It is the Camerlengo's understanding from talking to Pope John after they had all left, that Gabrielli had outlined to the Holy Father what he described as a three-stage plan, although the Camerlengo is unclear as to exactly what each stage comprised of. He believes that, as talking to the President had been so unsuccessful, stage one of Gabrielli's plan was to speak to the various women that the President was involved with instead, and to both ask and encourage them to cease their adulterous activities with the President. If these conversations were unsuccessful, then the Camerlengo's understanding was that Gabrielli then initiated stage two of his plan, which involved applying pressure on the women involved, but he is unaware of exactly what that pressure entailed.'

'I see,' said Pope Paul thoughtfully, 'and stage three?'

'We have no certain knowledge of exactly what stage three comprised of Holy Father, as the Camerlengo was kept completely in the dark of that aspect by Pope John. All he knew for certain was that stage three was only to be used if and when all other conceivable options had been tried and failed, and then only with the Holy Father's prior consent. It is the Camerlengo's firm belief that no such consent was ever given to Gabrielli, as Pope John tragically passed away before any such consent could even be considered. The Camerlengo believes that Gabrielli decided to go ahead with stage three anyway, acting on his own volition, believing that he was doing the then Holy Father's will. Obviously, there is no proof that such consent would have ever been given, or, for that matter, there is no proof that there ever was such a thing as a stage three.'

'And you believe, Signor Cavalli, that this "stage three" of Gabrielli's you keep referring to, was, in fact, the assassination of President Kennedy?'

'I'm afraid I do, Holy Father,' he replied. 'In fact, Gabrielli confirmed as much to me when I accosted him in his hotel room after the assassination, but he refused to return to Rome and said he and his men would all be returning to their old lives, which I took to mean Sicily.'

'Is there any way this heinous act, for that is surely what it was, can ever be laid at the door of the Vatican, Signor?'

'I don't think so, Holy Father. We don't know for sure what exactly Pope John XXIII instructed Gabrielli to do. We, of course, have our suspicions, but there is no proof. Likewise, the Camerlengo doesn't know for sure, and he would never say anything anyway. As for witnesses? Well, Lee Harvey Oswald was the only person ever accused of killing President Kennedy, and in all the interviews he had with the police and the FBI, he never once mentioned any connection to the Vatican. If what Gabrielli tells me is correct, and I have no reason to disbelieve him, Oswald thought he was working under the authority of the CIA in order to remove a rogue President. Nobody can check with Oswald or ask him further questions now because Jack Ruby shot him dead two days later. We are told Ruby did so because he was so upset over the assassination of a President he loved and admired. Again, there is no link to the Vatican whatsoever as Ruby was not aware of who Gabrielli was when Gabrielli set him up. As for Gabrielli? Well, he and his men have all since disappeared, as I said, probably back to their former lives in Sicily, and I suspect we will never see or hear from any of them ever again. I believe Gabrielli has helped himself to a substantial amount of Vatican money, but we can hardly prosecute him without everything we want to remain hidden coming out. I think we can safely say, Holy Father, that there is no way the Vatican can be, or ever will be, linked to the assassination of President Kennedy.'

'In that case, Signor Cavalli, I thank you for all that you have done on behalf of the Vatican and also for me personally, but please, let that be the end of the matter, and may it never be mentioned again.'

THE END

234